GOSSAMER

Power Crystal

Once a Star Darling has granted her first wish
and returns to Starland, she receives a very
special treasure—a beautiful Power Crystal.

BROOCH

Wish Pendant

A Wish Pendant is a powerful accessory worn
by a Star Darling. On Wishworld, it helps
her identify her Wisher and stores the
ever-important wish energy.

Tessa's Lost and Found

Tessa's Lost
and Found

Shana Muldoon Zappa and Ahmet Zappa

with Zelda Rose

DISNEP Press

Los Angeles • New York

Printed in the United States of America
Reinforced Binding
First Paperback Edition, May 2016
1 3 5 7 9 10 8 6 4 2

FAC-025438-16078

Library of Congress Control Number: 2015958597
ISBN 978-1-4847-1428-7

For more Disney Press fun, visit www.disneybooks.com

SUSTAINABLE
FORESTRY
INITIATIVE

Certified Chain of Custody
Promoting Sustainable Forestry

www.sfiprogram.org
SFI-01054

The SFI label applies to the text stock

Halo Violetta Zappa. You are pure light, joy, and inspiration. We love you soooooo much.

May the Star Darlings continue to shine brightly upon you. May every step upon your path be blessed with positivity and the understanding that you have the power within you to manifest the most fulfilling life you can possibly dream of and more. May you always remember that being different and true to yourself makes your inner star shine brighter. And never ever stop making wishes.

Glow for it. . . .
Mommy and Daddy

And to everyone else here on "Wishworld":

May you realize that no matter where you are in life, no matter what you look like or where you were born, you, too, have the power within you to create the life of your dreams. Through celebrating your own uniqueness, thinking positively, and taking action, you can make your wishes come true. May you understand that you are never alone. There is always someone near who will understand you if you look hard enough. The Star Darlings are here to remind you that there is an unstoppable energy to staying positive, wishing, and believing in yourself. That inner star shines within you.

Smile. The Star Darlings have your back. We know how startastic you truly are.

Glow for it. . . .
Your friends,
Shana and Ahmet

Student Reports

NAME: Clover
BRIGHT DAY: January 5
FAVORITE COLOR: Purple
INTERESTS: Music, painting, studying
WISH: To be the best songwriter and DJ on Starland
WHY CHOSEN: Clover has great self-discipline, patience, and willpower. She is creative, responsible, dependable, and extremely loyal.
WATCH OUT FOR: Clover can be hard to read and she is reserved with those she doesn't know. She's afraid to take risks and can be a wisecracker at times.
SCHOOL YEAR: Second
POWER CRYSTAL: Panthera
WISH PENDANT: Barrette

* * * * * * * * * * * *

NAME: Adora
BRIGHT DAY: February 14
FAVORITE COLOR: Sky blue
INTERESTS: Science, thinking about the future and how she can make it better
WISH: To be the top fashion designer on Starland
WHY CHOSEN: Adora is clever and popular and cares about the world around her. She's a deep thinker.
WATCH OUT FOR: Adora can have her head in the clouds and be thinking about other things.
SCHOOL YEAR: Third
POWER CRYSTAL: Azurica
WISH PENDANT: Watch

* * * * * * * * * * * *

NAME: Piper
BRIGHT DAY: March 4
FAVORITE COLOR: Seafoam green
INTERESTS: Composing poetry and writing in her dream journal
WISH: To become the best version of herself she can possibly be and to share that by writing books
WHY CHOSEN: Piper is giving, kind, and sensitive. She is very intuitive and aware.
WATCH OUT FOR: Piper can be dreamy, absentminded, and wishy-washy. She can also be moody and easily swayed by the opinions of others.
SCHOOL YEAR: Second
POWER CRYSTAL: Dreamalite
WISH PENDANT: Bracelets

Starling Academy

NAME: Libby
BRIGHT DAY: October 12
FAVORITE COLOR: Pink
INTERESTS: Helping others, interior design, art, dancing
WISH: To give everyone what they need—both on Starland and through wish granting on Wishworld
WHY CHOSEN: Libby is generous, articulate, gracious, diplomatic, and kind.
WATCH OUT FOR: Libby can be indecisive and may try too hard to please everyone.
SCHOOL YEAR: First
POWER CRYSTAL: Charmelite
WISH PENDANT: Necklace

* * * * * * * *

NAME: Scarlet
BRIGHT DAY: November 3
FAVORITE COLOR: Black
INTERESTS: Crystal climbing (and other extreme sports), magic, thrill seeking
WISH: To live on Wishworld
WHY CHOSEN: Scarlet is confident, intense, passionate, magnetic, curious, and very brave.
WATCH OUT FOR: Scarlet is a loner and can alienate others by being secretive, arrogant, stubborn, and jealous.
SCHOOL YEAR: Third
POWER CRYSTAL: Ravenstone
WISH PENDANT: Boots

* * * * * * * *

NAME: Sage
BRIGHT DAY: December 1
FAVORITE COLOR: Lavender
INTERESTS: Travel, adventure, telling stories, nature, and philosophy
WISH: To become the best Wish-Granter Starland has ever seen
WHY CHOSEN: Sage is honest, adventurous, curious, optimistic, friendly, and relaxed.
WATCH OUT FOR: Sage has a quick temper! She can also be restless, irresponsible, and too trusting of others' opinions. She may jump to conclusions.
SCHOOL YEAR: First
POWER CRYSTAL: Lavenderite
WISH PENDANT: Necklace

Introduction

You take a deep breath, about to blow out the candles on your birthday cake. Clutching a coin in your fist, you get ready to toss it into the dancing waters of a fountain. You stare at your little brother as you each hold an end of a dried wishbone, about to pull. But what do you do first?

You make a wish, of course!

Ever wonder what happens right after you make that wish? *Not much*, you may be thinking.

Well, you'd be wrong.

Because something quite unexpected happens next. Each and every wish that is made becomes a glowing Wish Orb, invisible to the human eye. This undetectable orb zips through the air and into the heavens, on a one-way trip to the brightest star in the sky—a magnificent place called Starland. Starland is inhabited by Starlings, who look a lot like you and me, except they have a sparkly glow to their skin, and glittery hair in unique colors. And they have one more thing: magical powers. The Starlings use these powers to make good wishes come true, for when good wishes are granted, the result is positive energy. And the Starlings of Starland need this energy to keep their world running.

In case you are wondering, there are three kinds of Wish Orbs:

1) GOOD WISH ORBS. These wishes are positive and helpful and come from the heart. They are pretty and sparkly and are nurtured in climate-controlled Wish-Houses. They bloom into fantastical glowing orbs. When the time is right, they are presented to the appropriate Starling for wish fulfillment.

2) BAD WISH ORBS. These are for selfish, mean-spirited, or negative things. They don't sparkle

at all. They are immediately transported to a special containment center, as they are very dangerous and must not be granted.

3) IMPOSSIBLE WISH ORBS. These wishes are for things, like world peace and disease cures, that simply can't be granted by Starlings. These sparkle with an almost impossibly bright light and are taken to a special area of the Wish-House with tinted windows to contain the glare they produce. The hope is that one day they can be turned into good wishes the Starlings can help grant.

Starlings take their wish granting very seriously. There is a special school, called Starling Academy, that accepts only the best and brightest young Starling girls. They study hard for four years, and when they graduate, they are ready to start traveling to Wishworld to help grant wishes. For as long as anyone can remember, only graduates of wish-granting schools have ever been allowed to travel to Wishworld. But things have changed in a very big way.

Read on for the rest of the story. . . .

Prologue

Curled up in bed, Tessa gazed at her Star-Zap screen and yawned. Her roommate, Adora, had been sleeping for at least a starhour. But Tessa needed to get a holo-mail out on the school's zap-app 3C, otherwise known as the Cosmic Communication Center.

The system had mail, calendars, announcements, holo-textbooks, and grades that were constantly updating. Right then, Tessa was writing to her Wishworld Relations teacher, asking for an extension on a holo-paper.

Tessa added a few words, then abandoned the holo-mail once again to peek at her grades in a different class, Wish Fulfillment. Maybe the stars had aligned and Professor Eugenia Bright had changed her grade since the last time she'd checked, about fifteen starmins earlier. No, there it was, exactly the same as before: A for *almost glowing*, two grades below the perfect I for *illumination*. Definitely not what she was aiming for!

Really, though, Wish Fulfillment was the least of Tessa's concerns. She had to focus on Wishworld Relations. But first she decided to check the scores for the Glowin' Glions star ball team and see how Astra had fared in the latest game.

"Moonberries!" she moaned. They'd lost to the Twinkling Twinkelopes by half a hydrong. Next she scrolled through some announcements.

"That's interesting," Tessa said out loud. The Star Darlings band's biggest rival was holding another audition. *And no wonder*, she thought, a little gleefully. Another Starling must have quit the group. A girl named Vivica was its leader. And no Starling with even a flounce of talent would stick with her band. The way Vivica and her friends treated others was downright mean.

Now what? Tessa wondered. What should she click on next? *Oh! That Wishworld Relations holo-mail!*

This time, for sure, she wouldn't get distracted. She'd finish the letter. But first she read over what she'd already written.

Star greetings, Professor Margaret Dumarre,

Hmmm . . . She hadn't gotten as far she'd thought! She nibbled one of the astromuffins she kept by her bedside, and in a burst of energy continued:

I'm writing this holo-letter while everyone else is sleeping. I should be sleeping, too, but I'm staying up late trying to finish my holo-paper, "Being Human." Of course I know that Wishlings call themselves human! I've known that since I was in Wee Constellation School. And as a third-year student, I've recently learned many of these "teenage humans" put off homework and studying so they can watch a screen called "television" and constantly check their low-tech devices: computers, tablets, and cell phones.

I've absorbed this information so well I seem to have developed some of these traits myself. I've put off this paper, and now with star apologies, I must tell you it's going to be late. Would it be possible to have an extension? Maybe another starweek, until next Dododay?

I don't mean to make star excuses, but unlike my Wishworld counterparts, I have valid reasons for being so late.

First, there's that ~~super-secret Star Darlings class we take to prepare for our wish missions~~ special class I have to take for extra help. It requires a lot of outside-the-classroom work. And I can't always judge the timing. Often Lady Stella calls us together unexpectedly. And sometimes we meet on our own. Just the other starday, we talked about ~~all the strange happenings on campus and on Starland.~~ the basics of a successful Wish Mission.

Specifically, we discussed:

~~How Lady Stella tells us there's nothing to worry about, but Starland has had several blackouts.~~
How to recognize that you have correctly identified your Wisher.

~~How Scarlet was kicked out of the SD group and replaced by Ophelia. When it turned out Ophelia desperately needed Scarlet's help, Lady Stella explained that Scarlet was back in and Ophelia was out. And most shockingly, how~~

~~Ophelia later disappeared and just told us that~~ ~~she was lying the whole time and that Lady~~ ~~Stella put her up to it.~~

How to ask probing, yet innocent questions to determine your Wisher's wish.

~~How all the SD roommates were fighting~~ ~~because of the poisonous flowers someone~~ ~~mysteriously placed in our rooms.~~

How to keep an eye on your Countdown Clock so you don't miss your wish window.

~~How Star Kindness Day was ruined by~~ ~~negative energy when holo-texted compliments~~ ~~were replaced by insults.~~

How to erase your Wisher's memory once the wish is granted and wish energy successfully collected.

~~How all the Star Darlings were acting odd~~ ~~because we were wearing special nail polish,~~ ~~probably made with negative energy. My~~ ~~reaction: everything tasted like moonberries.~~

How to return to Starland safely when your mission is accomplished.

There's so much material to cover, in fact, the
girls have an early-morning meeting in my room. ~~The
future of the Star Darlings~~ Our grades may hang in the
balance!

Starfully yours,
Tessa

And with those last words written and her real
thoughts deleted, Tessa finally fell asleep.

CHAPTER
1

The next morning should have worked out perfectly for Tessa. All the Star Darlings were coming to her and Adora's room for an important meeting. And she was totally prepared.

Even though she'd stayed up late working on her holo-paper—and excuse note—Tessa had set the alarm on her Star-Zap for an extra-early wake-up time. Before morning, the alarm buzzed her favorite childhood tune, "Old MacStarlight Had a Farm."

She took her sparkle shower in record time, not losing track of starmins the way she usually did. She finished so quickly, in fact, Adora was still sleeping soundly when she went back to the room.

So Tessa tidied her ultra-plush bedcovers and smoothed her soft-as-a-cloud rug. Both came from Bed, Bath, and Beyond the Stars' exclusive line of luxury items, perfect for Tessa, who liked to surround herself with sumptuous comfort.

Then she pulled on the outfit she'd laid out the night before: an emerald-green and ocean-blue striped sweaterdress that swirled around her knees. It matched Tessa's long wavy hair perfectly.

Quickly, Tessa checked her Star-Zap to make sure she was still on schedule. Yes, she was doing great. She picked up her starbrush to sweep her bangs to the side. There was just one more thing to do before the Star Darlings came over. She had to—

Tessa caught sight of the headboard over her bed . . . and everything fell apart.

The headboard was really one big holo-screen, and Tessa was drawn to it like solar metal to a magnet.

Initially, Tessa had used the screen to care for virtual pets. She loved creatures of all sizes, shapes, and glows. But then she'd programmed the screen to show her family farm in real time—real creatures in real action.

Tessa and her younger sister, Gemma—also a Star Darling—were from Solar Springs, a tiny town of gently rolling hills. A small number of families lived on simple farms nestled in valleys. It was a lovely spot. But the town had just one general store that sold only basic items, like toothlights and starbrushes.

When Tessa wanted that starmazing luster-lotion for her skin, or the glitz gloves that felt soft as shimmer-butter, she had to put in a special order. Except for that, Tessa loved her farm life: the fresh fruits and vegetables she used for cooking, the farm creatures . . .

And that was why she couldn't turn away from the screen. Her favorite creature of all, a playful baby gal-liope named Jewel, was there in all her cuteness, nudging a round druderwomp bush across the ground like a ball.

The deep purple creature was all spindly legs and long neck, with a glowing feathery mane and tail. Tessa had seen holo-pictures of Wishworld ponies. She agreed they resembled galliopes. But she doubted they could hold a glowstick to Jewel in charm alone.

Tessa dropped her starbrush and edged closer to the holo-screen. "Jewel," she cooed softly. "Star greetings, little girl."

If Jewel was in the right mood, she could step out of the screen—or at least her image could—and be virtually close to Tessa. Hoping that would happen, Tessa tapped the bottom of the screen, and a virtual starapple floated into her hand. She held out the sparkling round fruit to Jewel. Back on the farm, it wouldn't be just an image; the starapple would be real and crunchy and sweet.

Jewel whinnied, stepped out of the screen, and nuzzled Tessa's neck. "I could do this all starday," Tessa said with a giggle.

"Maybe you could, but you really shouldn't," said Adora. Tessa looked across the room. Adora had gotten up and dressed without her even noticing.

"Everyone will be here in a starsec. So pick up your starbrush and finish getting ready."

Tessa ignored her, putting her arm around Jewel. "I don't like being told what to do," she whispered, as if the galliope could understand. "You'd think after rooming together for so long, Adora would know that."

Sighing, Adora picked up Tessa's starbrush and placed it on the nightstand. "Come on, Tessa, I put away all my test tubes and experiments—even that new lip-sparkle I'm working on. The one that actually shoots out sparks."

Adora spoke as calmly as ever; Tessa had rarely seen her ruffled or emotional. And they generally got along.

But Tessa had cleaned up! What was one little starbrush in the grand scheme of things? Still, the Star Darlings were coming over. . . .

Tessa waved good-bye to Jewel, and the galliope stepped back into the screen. "See you soon, little girl. Next time we'll play and we'll—"

"Starland to Tessa!" Adora snapped her fingers in front of Tessa's face. "The Star Darlings meeting is—"

"*Knock-knock,*" sang Leona from the other side of the door.

"Now!" Adora finished, nodding toward the door so it slid open quickly. The other ten Star Darlings walked into the room and settled on beds, chairs, and rugs.

"Oh, Tessa," Gemma said, disappointment in her voice. She eyed Tessa's cleared-off table. "I thought for sure you'd have a whole breakfast spread for us."

Tessa groaned. That was what she'd been planning to do! Before she was distracted by Jewel, she had been about to bake breakfast treats in the micro-zap!

Scarlet shook her head emphatically, her dark hood falling to her shoulders before she quickly pulled it back up. "Breakfast is not important," she said brusquely. "We'll have plenty of time to go to the Celestial Café after the meeting."

"Still, we could have met a little later," Piper said wistfully, covering up a yawn. Tessa knew Piper liked her rest more than the average Starling.

"No, meeting now makes the most sense," said Vega. "This way we take care of business and keep the rest of the starday free for studying."

"I would have voted for a bit later so I'd have had time to warm up my vocal cords." Leona's voice started out deep, then rose higher with every word: "Now I have to do my exercises in regular conversation."

"Please, spare us," Scarlet said.

Tessa sighed. Those roommates were a much bigger mismatch than she and Adora! She doubted they would ever get along.

Cassie held up a hand, and everyone quieted down. She was the smallest Starling of the group, but her words carried great weight. "The fact is, spies could be any-where on campus. I don't know whom we can even trust! Not even Lady Stella."

Tessa laughed. "You don't really believe what that crazy Ophelia said, do you? She was clearly making it up."

Half the Star Darlings nodded in agreement. Others didn't look quite so convinced.

Libby stood up. "Okay, everybody, let's focus!"

Tessa nodded in agreement. It would also be great if they could move the meeting along so they could make it to breakfast in a timely fashion. Without her usual pre-breakfast snack, she was hungry.

"Fine." Cassie nodded. She took off her star-shaped glasses, polished them so they shone, and nodded again. "Someone is clearly trying to sabotage the Star Darlings. If it isn't Lady Stella, then who is it? And why? I mean, there have been so many crazy problems. . . ."

"Like our holo-text compliments coming out as insults," interrupted Piper indignantly.

"And every student invited to try out for my band," Leona added, "when it should have just been Star -Darlings!"

"And those are just communication issues," Cassie continued. "What about everything else? The poisonous flowers? The strange nail polish that wouldn't come off? Who is responsible?"

Scarlet shook her head irritably. "It's so clearly Lady Stella," she said. "Why can't you all see it?"

The Star Darlings began to argue.

Lady Stella was the head of the school. She was revered in academic circles for her principles and forward thinking in education. She was held in highest regard all across Starland. Business Starlings, Starling scientists, and heads of state constantly consulted her, and wee Starlings wanted to grow up to be just like her.

Tessa had actually dressed as Lady Stella once for Light Giving Day, when young Starlings dressed in costume to hand out flowers and welcome the growing season. She guessed a couple of others may have, too.

Tessa thought back to one of her first days at the academy, well before the Star Darlings had been formed. She had been curled up in a chair in the Lightning Lounge, holo-texting Gemma back home and feeling homesick.

Lady Stella had come over and sat down next to her. She seemed to know all about Tessa without Tessa's saying a word, and she led her on a tour of the Celestial Café kitchen, where Bot-Bot cooks and waitstaff worked.

"You can come here any time you like," she had said, "and cook, bake, or just relax. The Bot-Bots will be informed."

Then they'd sat in a corner and munched on astromuffins together—moonberry for Lady Stella (she said they were her favorite) and lolofruit for Tessa.

Lady Stella couldn't be capable of any wrongdoing whatsoever!

"Scarlet, you're going galactic!" said Libby, apparently agreeing with Tessa. "The person or people responsible don't even have to be part of Starling Academy! He or she could be from outside the school."

"I doubt that," Cassie said nervously. "Whoever is doing this would need to be here full-time. And Lady Stella is here 36/8."

"You're *both* going galactic!" Sage said to Scarlet and Cassie. "Lady Stella has been starmendous to each and every one of us!"

"Well, count me out of that lucky stargroup," Scarlet shot back. "Here's a fact for you: my grades were switched with dimwit Ophelia's so I'd be kicked out of the Star Darlings. Who else would be able to do that? And why would Ophelia lie?"

The girls fell silent. It was hard to disagree with Scarlet; plus, she could so easily go supernova. Tessa looked at Leona, who stood up to Scarlet regularly. But Leona had been uncharacteristically quiet. Then Tessa glanced at Gemma. What was her sister thinking? She, too, had been quiet.

"Well, lots of Starlings could have access to records,"

Tessa finally said. "What about the Bot-Bot guards? They have access to every room on campus."

Gemma finally spoke up. "That's right! Once, when I was walking past the teachers' lounge, I was hurrying really fast down the hall. I can't even remember why I was there. Maybe because I had to go to the Radiant Rec Center and I was a little nervous because I had never—"

"Get to the point of the story," said Scarlet.

"Well, once there was a Bot-Bot repairman outside the lounge door, stooping over. He could have been try-ing to listen in!"

"Or fix the hand scanner," said Scarlet.

"Lady Cordial keeps close watch on all the com-ings and goings in that hall," Cassie noted, "because the admissions office is there. She'd notice anything strange. So forget about the Bot-Bot!" She sighed. "Lady Stella clearly set up the whole Scarlet-Ophelia switch. She told me Ophelia was an orphan. She lied. And as we all know, Ophelia was never even in an orphanage!"

Scarlet leaned closer to Sage with an almost compas-sionate expression. "I was fooled, too, for a long time." A shadow passed over her face. "But Lady Stella pulled the glimmersilk over my eyes."

Finally, Leona spoke up, as if she'd been weigh-ing the information and had made up her mind. "Well,

I spent the most time with Ophelia of all of you, and frankly, I think she's telling the truth."

"But why would Lady Stella want to sabotage our missions?" Vega asked. "It doesn't make sense. The missions were her idea to begin with!"

The girls all spoke at once.

"Maybe she wants Starling Academy to fail so she can start a new school."

"Maybe she wants to move to Wishworld!"

"Maybe she's just a hologram, and the real Lady Stella is being held captive in one of the underground caves."

Tessa shivered. The last comment, which had come from Piper, was especially creepy.

"I don't know why she's doing it," said Scarlet. "But we have to confront her, and soon."

"I just don't believe it," said Tessa stubbornly. "I need real proof."

"I don't believe it, either," Sage said.

The room fell silent. The girls eyed each other nervously. No one knew what to say. But then Tessa's stomach rumbled loudly. Gemma laughed, breaking the tension.

"I say we've talked enough for now. It's time to eat," said Tessa.

Cassie nodded and stood up. "Before we confront

anyone," she said to Scarlet, "we should do more sleuthing." Then she turned to Tessa. "And you're right, of course. We should all go to breakfast."

Cassie is smart, Tessa thought as everyone left the room, *even if she does suspect Lady Stella. And she's read all those detective books her uncle wrote; she must know about sleuthing.* She'd stick close to Cassie, find out what was really going on, and put in her two stars to defend Lady Stella whenever she could.

Tessa stepped onto the Cosmic Transporter, careful to get in place right behind the younger Starling.

Cassie and Scarlet were standing side by side, whispering. Tessa edged closer, trying to listen. *It's not like I'm really eavesdropping*, she reasoned. *We're all just heading to the Celestial Café at the same time.*

But all she heard was: "Mumble mumble Lady Stella." "Mumble mumble Leona." "Mumble Ophelia." "Mumble mumble mumble."

Nothing new there.

Then Cassie said "Star Caves" loud and clear. Scarlet gave her a "shut your stars" look. "Later!" the older Starling whispered harshly.

Hmmm, thought Tessa. Now that was interesting. They must think the secret underground tunnels, where the special Star Darlings Wish Cavern was hidden, held clues. *Maybe—*

Suddenly, the star above the Celestial Café dimmed, signaling that breakfast was about to end. Tessa forgot about the caves. She took off past the other Starlings, thoughts of warm astromuffins and tinsel toast filling her head.

CHAPTER
2

After breakfast, Tessa's starday was basically back-to-back classes. Some flew by like a comet. Others seemed to last an entire Cycle of Life. So much of what the professors taught had already been covered in the special Star Darlings class.

Tessa's final class before Star Darlings lessons was Wish Fulfillment, taught by Professor Eugenia Bright. Usually, Tessa paid attention to Professor Bright's lessons; the teacher was warm and engaging and cared about each student. Besides, Tessa wanted to raise her grade.

That day Professor Bright was lecturing about wish fulfillment history: how Starlandians had first discovered their connection to Wishworld.

"During a space exploration trip," the teacher explained, "scientist Dusty Particulus forgot to transfer shooting stars. She wound up landing near a group of Wishling stargazers just as they wished on a different shooting star. One Wishling said, 'I wish I could come face-to-face with someone from another planet.' So Dusty stepped right in front of her, and suddenly a surge of energy..."

Yes, it was starmazingly interesting. But Tessa had heard the story so many times she found her mind wandering back to the Star Darlings meeting.

It was true: much had gone wrong for the Star Darlings. Right there on Starland, there had been the band tryouts, the flowers, the nail polish, the holo-texts, and, of course, the power failures that affected the whole planet. And they'd had trouble on Wishworld, too. There had been Leona's burnt-out Wish Pendant that lost wish energy; and her scary trip back, when she almost hadn't made it home; and all the Starlings' misidentifying of Wishers and wishes.

But Lady Stella? How could some of the Star Darlings think she was responsible?

"Star excuse me, Tessa." Tessa looked up. Professor Eugenia Bright was standing over her desk, smiling. They were the only two in the classroom.

"Is there something you'd like to discuss with me?" the teacher asked kindly.

Tessa eyed the professor. She had to say something, but she certainly couldn't say she'd been lost in thought, wondering if Lady Stella was sabotaging Starland.

"I like your earrings!" she sputtered. She turned deep green with embarrassment, but it was true—she did like them! The glittery cylinders hung almost to Professor Bright's shoulders and twirled when she moved, giving off sparks. They were exquisite and classic and must have come from Starland's most acclaimed jewelry store, Starrier's, where the rich and famous shopped.

Professor Eugenia Bright lowered her voice. "I found them at the Brilliant Bargain Basement in Old Prism. Sure, it's a tourist town, but you can still find starmazing deals there."

Tessa laughed and stopped worrying about Lady Stella and Star Darlings problems—at least for the moment.

★

That afternoon, Tessa joined the Future Farmers of Starland after-school club. They visited a new colony of glitterbees at the foot of the Crystal Mountains. And it was well worth the trip, Tessa thought on the way back. One delicatacomb in particular was starmendous, as big as a Starcar! Plus, she even managed to bring some of the sweet liquid back to campus. It was starrific for baking.

But now, standing in front of Halo Hall, saying good-bye to her fellow future farmers, Tessa felt restless. She paced back and forth, her mind returning again and again to Lady Stella. She thought fleetingly of her overdue Wishworld Relations paper. She even took a few tentative steps toward the library. But how could she settle down to work when her mind was in such a state?

Tessa's feet switched course and she found herself heading to the Celestial Café.

I'll just bake for a starhour or so, Tessa thought. *It will calm me down, help me focus, and then* . . . "On to my 'Being Human' paper!"

"You're still working on that?" Cassie asked. Tessa hadn't realized that she'd spoken out loud, or that Cassie was walking next to her. She shook her head to clear it. She really did need to bake!

"Yes, but cross my stars, I'll get an extension. I'm still waiting to hear from Professor Margaret Dumarre. Right now I'm going to the kitchen."

Cassie brightened, and her pale skin glittered, showing her interest. "Are you baking? Can I tag along? I promise I won't talk about Lady Stella. We can agree to disagree until more facts are in."

"Of course!" It would be an opportunity to find out about the caves with Cassie. Usually when she baked, every bit of her energy went into creating the perfect dish. But this time, she'd multitask. Smiling, she motioned for Cassie to join her as she stepped off the Cosmic Transporter.

"I want to use fresh delicata," Tessa went on, "so I'm thinking about mini comet cakes. Only instead of sparkleberries, I might add cocomoons with a starburst of solar cream."

"Mmm-mmm," said Cassie as they entered the kitchen. "Sounds starmendous. What can I do to help?"

"For starters, set the micro-zap for a moonium and four degrees."

The two girls got to work, Tessa humming as she measured and mixed, crimped and coated, sometimes telling Cassie what to add.

"A flounce of milk."

"Two quax of sunflour."

"A zingspoon of sparklesugar."

Then she poured the batter and popped the tray

into the micro-zap. "Two point six seven starsecs," she instructed Cassie. She grinned happily. "Star salutations for your help!" Then she remembered: the whole time, she was supposed to have been getting more information!

Before she could say anything else, the comet cakes were ready. There were twelve mini comet cakes, one for each Star Darling. Tessa couldn't help admiring the treats, with their perfectly round shape and tapered tails made from starberries. The bright red fruit looked just like a comet's fiery stream.

Cassie sniffed. "They smell so good! Can I have mine now?"

Tessa grinned. "Tell you what. Let's have as many as we want. Then we can make another batch!"

Cassie stretched out her hand, but Tessa held the tray high over the small Starling's head. It was a little unfair, she knew, to hold back the treat. But she had to work fast now to get some information. And she knew from when Gemma was younger that this was the best way to get it.

"Tell me what you and Scarlet were whispering about on the Cosmic Transporter this morning."

"What? I don't know what you mean," Cassie said, turning away so she wouldn't have to look Tessa in the eye.

"Oh, I think you do." Tessa sounded more confident

than she felt. "I distinctly heard you say 'Star Caves.' And I bet you two are convinced those caves have something to do with your Lady Stella suspicions."

The caves were real, not a theory or an idea, and they were something Tessa could reach out and touch—something that could hold solid proof of Lady Stella's innocence. *Or guilt,* Tessa thought for a starsec, before she could help herself.

She lowered the tray and waved it tantalizingly under Cassie's nose.

"Oh, okay!" Cassie grabbed a cake.

She paused to take a bite. "Scarlet's explored the caves. She found another entrance, and she's gone down a bunch of times. I guess she likes the bitbats and the feel of the tunnels—the mystery and the isolation. But it's not as if she's found anything revealing there."

"Is that all?" Tessa asked, disappointed.

"Well, I have my own ideas about the caves," Cassie went on. "There are so many twists and turns. They could hold so many secrets, and they're so closely tied to our missions I just feel there could be clues down there—answers to what's been going on."

"Exactly!" Tessa exclaimed. "So what are you two going to do next? For your sleuthing?"

"Nothing," said Cassie, squirming a bit.

Was Cassie skirting the truth? She seemed uncomfortable, and Tessa guessed the Starling didn't really like to lie. So she didn't want to call her on it. But she needed to keep pressing her.

"The next time Scarlet explores the caves, we should go, too," Tessa said. "We may spot something she's missed."

Tessa gave a little shudder. Really, the last thing she wanted to do was trek through those damp, spooky tunnels. Going with the Star Darlings to their special Wish Cavern was one thing. But just roaming around—unescorted—was a galliope of an entirely different color.

Meanwhile, Cassie had polished off four comet cakes and was reaching for a fifth. "Well, I can ask her. I have no idea what she'll say, though, and there's no way we can go alone. We don't even know how to get in."

Cassie popped the round cake into her mouth and sighed. "These are really good, Tessa. I wish I could bake like you."

"You can!" said Tessa. "You already watched me once. So this time when I bake, holo-vid me with your Star-Zap and use it for reference."

"Can I borrow yours?" asked Cassie. "I brought

mine in for repairs. It's been weird lately, and I haven't been able to get holo-messages, or even send them."

"Uh-huh," Tessa murmured, not really listening. Already she was measuring sparklesugar and pouring it into a bowl. Maybe this time she'd add just a flicker more delicata. . . .

CHAPTER
3

The next starday Tessa was late for class. But why, oh, why did it have to be Wishworld Relations with Professor Margaret Dumarre?

After baking the comet cakes with Cassie, she'd felt so calm and productive she'd actually finished her "Being Human" paper. She'd sent it right off but hadn't heard back from the professor. Not a holo-note saying it was okay it was late. Not a message saying she was lowering the grade because Tessa had missed the due date. However her teacher felt, Tessa wasn't looking forward to walking into class after the lecture had already begun.

If only she hadn't tried to take a quick peek at Jewel! The "quick peek" had turned into a very long gaze. And then her mom had holo-texted a new recipe, and Tessa just had to holo-call to say star salutations, it sounded great, and the two had talked until her mom asked why she wasn't in class.

Now, racing along the Cosmic Transporter, she was tempted to go back to her room and grab a leftover comet cake to give to Professor Margaret Dumarre. Maybe that would somehow explain her tardiness, or at least give the teacher a reason to be more lenient. But Tessa doubted that would, in fact, help. Professor Margaret Dumarre would know she was being bribed.

"Oops!" Lost in thought, Tessa had almost gone right by her classroom.

"Hey, where's the starfire?" Scarlet stepped in front of her, blocking the classroom door.

"I'm late for class, Scarlet. So please star excuse me." Tessa started to walk around the other Starling, but then she remembered the caves. She stopped, turned back, and smiled encouragingly.

Scarlet almost smiled back. "I'm actually late, too. Since I've stopped skipping, it's taking me longer to get places than I think it should." She shrugged. "I didn't even know I was skipping, but I guess acting crazy can have its benefits. Anyway, it's okay with me if you and Cassie come with me next time."

"To the caves?" Tessa said loudly, not quite hiding her

surprise. It was all happening faster than she'd thought it would. She had imagined Cassie would have trouble convincing Scarlet, a notorious loner, to let them go along.

"Shhh!" Scarlet said, annoyed. Then she stomped away without saying another word, her boots thudding loudly.

Tessa took a deep breath and peered through the window of the classroom door. Professor Margaret Dumarre had her back to Tessa and was speaking to the students.

Now! thought Tessa. She quietly opened the door—just a bit—with her wish energy manipulation, then slipped inside.

"Today we will delve into one of the pillars of positivity: creating a peaceful space." Professor Margaret Dumarre paused, then, with her back still to Tessa, said, "Tessa, please take a seat and join us."

Tessa hurried to an empty desk, thinking, *That wasn't bad at all!* Professor Margaret Dumarre didn't sound angry in the least. Maybe she didn't care that Tessa was arriving after the bell.

A girl named Violetta, sitting next to Tessa, turned to her with a smirk. "Late again, Star Dope," she hissed.

If only she hadn't been in such a rush, Tessa would have noticed Violetta and found another empty desk. She would never, in a moonium staryears, purposely sit next to the girl. The purple-haired Starling was great friends with Vivica. Even though Violetta was two grades ahead, she fawned over the younger Starling as if she was the most starmazing thing since sliced tinsel toast.

Maybe Violetta liked the way their names sounded together, or maybe she was just afraid if she didn't flatter Vivica, she would turn on Violetta like she had done to so many others.

Violetta tapped the clock on her Star-Zap and shook her head sadly at Tessa. "Now you're slow to get to class, too? Poor, poor Tessa. You Slow Developers lag behind in everything."

Or maybe she was just plain mean.

Tessa shifted her attention to the front of the room. Professor Margaret Dumarre was gesturing at a small device. Instantly, a holo-picture of a lovely garden appeared. Flutterfocuses, their sparkly wings glowing, fluttered around delicate blushbelle flowers, their pink petals glimmering in the sun. Kaleidoscope trees ringed a clear blue pond, their ever-changing colors reflected in the still waters.

With a wave of the teacher's arm, the picture expanded, wrapping around the classroom and winding among desks so it seemed the girls were sitting right at its very center.

Professor Margaret Dumarre wrinkled her forehead in concentration, her magenta-and-blue-striped bangs swaying gently with the motion. Tessa's seat slowly transformed, shrinking, changing shape, texture, and color, until she realized she was sitting on a moss-covered stone as soft as her bed. She looked around and saw all the chairs had been replaced. A sweet fragrance filled the air. Someone sighed with contentment.

"To feel positive, to be trusting and open to experience and accepting of outcomes, to be in the moment . . ." Professor Margaret Dumarre spoke in a low soothing voice. "Be mindful of your surroundings. Feel a sense of place . . . real or imagined. And let that place bring a peaceful moment . . . a moment that will bring good vibrations to everything and everyone in sight. Gather and share that positive energy flow!"

Tessa's fingers grazed her velvety-smooth moss and, using all her senses, took in the scene.

She watched a gold-and-silver flutterfocus intently, studying and enjoying its grace and beauty. She felt loose and relaxed.

Is this for real? she wondered idly. *Or just a holo-illusion?* The girl on her other side slowly tipped her head up to the ceiling, now a bright sky. The entire class seemed lulled into a sunshiny, dreamy state. Even Violetta had a sweet smile on her face. So maybe it didn't matter.

What counted was the feeling, the positive emotion you took from a tranquil setting—the feeling that you could achieve the impossible. She felt the positive energy flow.

"Creating a peaceful space," Professor Margaret Dumarre said softly, "can bring with it power to shrug off negativity."

She turned to look steadily toward Tessa, an understanding smile on her lips. "One day, when you're on a Wishworld mission, things may not be going your way. You may not be able to find your Wisher." She paused for a moogle to stare directly at Tessa. "Or your Wisher may be late."

Tessa realized she hadn't really gotten away with anything. In her own way, Professor Margaret Dumarre was taking her to task for being late. But Tessa felt surprisingly okay about it; the calm feeling persisted.

"And in those cases," the professor continued, "you'll need to increase your positivity."

At the word *positivity*, Tessa heard a buzzing sound and looked for a nearby glitterbee among the flowers. But the garden scene was fading, the flutterfocuses and flowers disappearing, and the buzzing seemed more insistent.

Oh! Tessa realized with a start that it was her Star-Zap, set on low.

"Class dismissed. See you on Lunaday," the teacher said, smiling. "And don't forget to check 3C for your term paper grades. I'm sure you'll all be pleased. There were many Is."

Illumination! Tessa thought. Did she have a moonshot at a grade like that? Violetta gave her one last sneer before she left class, saying, "If I were a Star Dope, I wouldn't be in a rush to find out my grades."

But Violetta spoke in such a soft, pleasant way the words barely stung. *Positivity at work!* Tessa thought. *A little more time spent in pleasant surroundings—minus Vivica—might be all that Starling needs.*

Buzzzz!

Oh, my Star-Zap, Tessa remembered. She checked the screen and saw a group holo-text from Scarlet, with Cassie included in the message.

 My Aspirational Art class is canceled! Professor Findley Claxworth is off to Starland City for the opening of his new exhibit, *Paint by Sunbursts.* Have free period next. Let's go exploring! Meet me at the fountain right now!

Tessa had to smile. Scarlet, usually so abrupt, was quite chatty by holo-text!

Luckily, Tessa had an independent study period next. She was supposed to go to the Illumination Library and report to the supervising librarian, Lady Floridia. But as a third year, she was allowed to skip study hall three times a term. She wasn't sure how many periods she'd missed already. Hadn't she used some study time to bake Bright Day cakes just recently?

But she didn't have time to check in at the Illumination Library, so she hurried directly to the fountain, in the Star Quad. As always, the water seemed to dance as it flowed, sparkling with all the colors of the rainbow. Scarlet was already there.

"Where's Cassie?" Scarlet said immediately, dispensing with any sort of greeting.

"*Moonberries!*" Tessa shook her head. "I totally forgot. Cassie brought her Star-Zap in for repairs. She didn't get the holo-text."

Tessa expected an angry retort from Scarlet, but maybe she'd come from a positivity class, too, because the Starling only shrugged. "Well, no rush. I have band practice after this period, but Leona won't mind if I skip it."

Scarlet was the Star Darlings band's drummer. She

was so talented maybe Leona allowed her flexibility. But no matter what, Leona most certainly *would* mind if Scarlet missed practice.

Then again, Scarlet probably found that appealing.

"Cassie has Wishers 101," Tessa told Scarlet. It was an introductory course, taught by Professor Elara Ursa. The class was held in the largest lecture hall, filled with row upon row of first years just figuring out Wishlings. Cassie had already met several in person and surely knew more than all the other students combined. It wouldn't be a big deal for her to miss it. "If we hurry, we can catch her before class starts."

The two Starlings ran along the Cosmic Transporter but weren't quite fast enough. Cassie's classroom door was just sliding shut as they approached. Through the door's window, they could see Cassie's pink hair falling over her desk as she readied her supplies.

"Come on," said Scarlet, pulling Tessa back outside. She stopped by the floor-to-ceiling window along one wall of the lecture hall. "We'll just wave to Cassie until she comes out."

"Uh, I don't think so."

The last teacher Tessa wanted to get in trouble with was Professor Elara Ursa. Well, no. The very last teacher was Professor Margaret Dumarre. But she needed to be on her best behavior around Professor Elara Ursa, too.

Tessa ducked behind a starmarble pillar.

"Listen, Tessa, you have to stop hiding," Scarlet told her. "You still haven't gone on a mission, so you may be chosen any starmin now. How will you be successful on Wishworld if you're too nervous to get a friend out of class right here on Starland?"

Tessa took a deep breath. Everyone knew Scarlet was fearless. And she, Tessa, was not—not by a moonshot. Still, Scarlet had a point. She had to learn to handle setbacks, just like Professor Margaret Dumarre was trying to teach them. For a moogle, she pictured the peaceful classroom garden.

"Okay," she said, stepping close to Scarlet.

Scarlet grinned, then waved her arms furiously at Cassie. She shielded her eyes like she was on some sort of search, then flapped her arms like a bitbat.

It was a good pantomime and would definitely give Cassie the idea of exploring the caves . . . if she was looking. Unfortunately, she wasn't.

Tessa waved tentatively just as Cassie turned her head and seemed to stare in her direction. So Tessa gestured widely with both arms, meaning, "Come out to us."

Cassie wrinkled her brow in a "Huh?" expression.

Now Tessa put her whole body into it, gesturing wildly at Cassie, then crouching low and holding her Star-Zap like a flashlight, as if she was exploring a dark tunnel. Tessa began to enjoy herself, thinking it was like star charades, a game she and Gemma would play for starhours on cold, snowy nights at the farm. She didn't even pause when Scarlet tapped her shoulder.

"Wait a moogle. I'm almost finished," she whispered.

"Finished doing what?" asked someone in an amused tone. It was a voice Tessa knew all too well. She straightened slowly, a bright green blush rising to her cheeks.

"Uh, nothing, Professor Elara Ursa," she said weakly. Scarlet was nowhere to be seen.

"Would you mind doing 'nothing' somewhere else, Tessa?" the professor said pleasantly. "It's a little distracting for the class."

"Of course," said Tessa, edging away and ducking her head in embarrassment. "Star apologies, Professor Elara Ursa."

When she found the courage to look at the teacher, it was too late. Professor Elara Ursa was already back in the classroom.

"Whew, that was close," said Scarlet, emerging from behind the pillar.

"Yes, for me," Tessa said testily. But really, she'd done

the same kind of thing to Gemma at home, thinking their parents would go easier on her little sister because she was younger. Of course, she and Scarlet were exactly the same star age. But what good did it do for both of them to get in trouble? "Now what?"

"We go to the caves!" said Cassie, coming out from behind the pillar, too. "While you were talking to Professor Elara Ursa, Scarlet snuck me out of class!"

⭐

"Wrong way, Tessa!"

"What?" Tessa was heading toward Lady Stella's office, where the Star Darlings always took a secret passage to the Star Caves.

"I said, wrong way," Scarlet repeated. Tugging on Tessa's arm, she led Tessa and Cassie out of the building, toward the dorms.

"Where exactly are we going?" asked Cassie.

"To the Big Dipper Dorm."

Cassie opened her mouth to ask another question, but Tessa shot her a look. Tessa was learning that sometimes with Scarlet, less was more. Not asking questions might get you all the info you needed.

"There's another entrance here," Scarlet continued,

leading them inside the dorm, then through the halls to a door marked STARLING ACADEMY STAFF ONLY.

"This is it?" Tessa asked. Her stomach rumbled, the way it did when she felt hungry—or anxious. She thought longingly of her room, only a few doors away, where a dish of garble green chips sat on her desk.

Without saying a word, Scarlet opened the door. Inside, Tessa saw a tiny room filled with baskets of glo-pong balls, sparkle-shower supplies, and disappearing garbage cans. The three girls stepped into the small space, and Scarlet shut the door behind them. They were in total darkness.

Tessa sucked in her breath and only released it when Scarlet switched her Star-Zap to flashlight mode. Scarlet flicked her wrist, and a trapdoor opened at their feet.

The supply closet filled with an eerie light. Tessa glimpsed winding metal stairs but nothing else. "Let's go," Scarlet whispered.

"Okay," Tessa whispered back. That was what she wanted, after all. She wanted to find something there that would clear Lady Stella or at least provide a clue.

Still, farm girl Tessa liked bright open spaces, not closed-in dimly lit tunnels. Of course she'd been in the caves many times and loved the light-filled Wish-House. But she'd never, ever enjoyed the trip there. And that was when Lady Stella had been leading the way. Now she and Cassie only had—*gulp!*—Scarlet.

As they made their way down the steps and into a passage, Tessa gazed at water dripping from the ceiling. Rocks hung like icicles, and stones rose from the ground in pointed shapes. Glowing gems, set deeply into walls, cast strange shadows. No, she really didn't want to be there.

But Scarlet seemed to know her way, walking quickly through corridor after corridor, stopping once to point the way to their secret Wish Cavern.

"I don't know what we're looking for." Cassie spoke for the first time in a quiet, calm voice.

"Me neither," said Scarlet almost happily. "But if Lady Stella is doing something in secret, it would probably be down here, in a spot the rest of us have never seen. Maybe there's a room full of poisonous flowers. Or a tech lab where she can mess with everyone's Star-Zaps.

"Besides," Scarlet went on, "isn't it a nice change of pace from being aboveground, surrounded by so many Starlings and their silly chatter? I feel like I can breathe here."

Tessa pulled out her Star-Zap. "I forgot to tell Gemma where I was going," she said.

Scarlet put her hand over the communicator. "Those don't work down here," she said.

Tessa didn't feel the way Scarlet did about being underground and was about to suggest they leave, when, suddenly, a bitbat swooped star inches from her face. Tessa jumped back, startled.

"Star greetings, little one," Scarlet said in a cooing voice Tessa had never heard her use before. The bitbat landed on Scarlet's outstretched finger, then swung upside down, folding its wings.

"Oh!" Tessa gasped. "She's so cute!" Tessa had never seen a bitbat so close before. She was silvery white and as small as a glowfur. Her big luminous green eyes seemed a little sad.

Tentatively, Tessa held out her hand, and the bitbat swung over to her finger.

"Ugh." Cassie pressed herself against the wall.

"She likes you, Tessa," said Scarlet approvingly.

Other bitbats flew past, and Tessa smiled. They were like tiny acrobats, somersaulting through the air and swaying upside down. "I like them, too!" she said.

Tessa felt her fears vanish into the air. She understood

now why Scarlet could spend starhours there.

They wandered the caves until it was time to go to their next class. The caves suddenly seemed enticing and mysterious to Tessa, and she felt like she understood Scarlet better after that. At least a little bit anyway.

But still, they didn't find a thing.

CHAPTER
4

The next morning, Tessa was the first to arrive at the Star Darlings' table in the Celestial Café. She turned to the door, and right on cue, Gemma walked in. The two were almost always the earliest for breakfast. Life on the farm began with the chickadoodles crowing at sunrise. And neither could manage to sleep even a bit past that—with few exceptions.

The sisters settled into seats facing the café's glass wall, with a glowrious view of the Crystal Mountains. Brilliant rays bounced off the mountain peaks. For a moogle, the two were silent. Even Gemma knew to sit quietly, soaking in the positive energy.

"So," Gemma said, finally breaking the silence, "I have to tell you what happened last starnight. Libby and

I were walking through the Serenity Gardens when we saw Piper meditating. So we . . ."

Tessa listened with one ear, a skill she'd developed at a young age when it became clear that Gemma could take starhours to tell a story that should be told in starmins. Their orders were taken and delivered. She finished her starcakes, then looked questioningly at Gemma and her half-eaten bowl of Sparkle-O's.

Nodding, Gemma pushed the bowl to her, saying, "So then Piper tells us this dream about driving a Starcar. I mean actually steering and braking it, with no auto feature that she can figure out, and . . ."

Meanwhile, more Star Darlings were arriving, and the café was filling with students eating, talking, and laughing. Leona, Piper, Astra, and the others sat down, with Scarlet slipping into a seat at the other end of the table. Only Cassie was missing then.

"Sage, did you see Cassie this morning?" Tessa asked.

Sage shook her head, tossing her long lavender hair. "No, she was already gone when I woke up."

Just then, Cassie hurried in, looking worried. She took the last seat, next to Scarlet.

"Is everything all right?" Tessa asked, her voice carrying across the table.

All talking stopped while everyone turned to Cassie. Even a few girls at the next table paused their conversation to listen. Tessa noted Vivica at the head of that table, Violetta at her side.

Cassie gave a funny sort of laugh. "Of course." She shot a look at the other table, and the girls reluctantly turned away. "I stopped by tech repair to pick up my Star-Zap. . . ." She trailed off as if she had more to say.

"And?" Sage asked impatiently.

"Well, it's fixed." Cassie leaned forward, lowering her voice. "But something strange may have happened to it."

"Something strange happened to your Star-Zap?" Tessa repeated to make sure she'd heard correctly. Heads turned in her direction. *Oh, starf.* She'd spoken way too loudly. Now everyone was interested.

So she raised her voice even louder. "I've heard about this new virus going around."

"Me too!" added Sage. "My mom was talking about it. The Star Bores bug. It just keeps replaying your old holo-texts."

"Oh, that's old news," Vivica called out loudly, not even caring that now everyone knew she'd been eavesdropping. "You Slow Developers are always behind the times. You should have a new special class, just for how to work a Star-Zap."

She and her friends giggled loudly, then flounced out of the café with superior looks at the Star Darlings.

"Don't let them dim your glow," Libby told Cassie. "Go on."

"Well," Cassie continued after taking a deep breath, "it turns out my messages were all being rerouted, stars know where. The technician said it might be a virus. Or a forwarding mechanism could have been—"

She whispered the rest of her sentence to Scarlet, who frowned and leaned over to whisper to Libby. Libby whispered to Sage, and the message went around the table until it reached Tessa.

"The forwarding mechanism could have been saving face on your jar cap?" Tessa giggled. "This is worse than a game of holo-phone!" she complained. "Let's find somewhere to talk."

So the entire group of Star Darlings got up and found a private relaxation room in the nearby Lightning Lounge. Immediately, the room started to play the theme song from a popular—and scary—weekly holo-vision program called *The Dark Files*. The show had been keeping viewers in suspense for eons. Tessa wasn't crazy about it; it was too spooky for her liking. Plus every starweek it focused on some strange conspiracy theory, such as all Starland leaders plotting with alien beings. For once she wished the room's sensors didn't pick up on mood.

But a few starmins later, Tessa finally understood what Cassie had been talking about: the technician thought someone might have sabotaged Cassie's Star-Zap, programming it to send her holo-texts to another device. Astra had a thoughtful look on her face. "Mine's been acting odd, too," she said.

"Remember when I accidentally left it in Lady Stella's office?" Cassie asked everyone. "She could have done something with it then."

"Oh, come on," Sage said, leaning back to gaze at the sky as the retractable roof opened. "First of all, Cassie, you're always losing your device. I can't count how many times you've had to use Find My Zap.

"Besides," she added offhandedly, "you always think people are taking it, too. Remember when you thought Lady Cordial, of all Starlings, stole it?"

All the Star Darlings giggled.

"When was that?" asked Libby. "Oh, right, during the first week of school."

Tessa remembered the Star Quad had been filled with first years who were having trouble getting acclimated to their Star-Zaps. Of course, poor Lady Cordial, the admissions director, had been in a panic. She was trying to explain how Star-Zaps worked to a large group. But her stuttering had been so severe no one could understand her.

"Yes," Cassie said, "somehow my device wound up with all her display Star-Zaps, and she was about to walk away with it! When I asked for it back, she was so distraught she tried to give me a different one! Then she offered to give me all the Star-Zaps!"

"Lady Cordial is always trying to do the right thing," Libby said. "Once she held the door open for Lady Stella using wish energy, but then Starlings kept coming and she didn't want to close it on anyone, so she stood there, concentrating on that door, for an entire starhour."

"I'm just saying it's possible," Cassie said, bringing the conversation back to Lady Stella's tampering with her Star-Zap. "Lady Stella isn't like Lady Cordial. She's so powerful. Everyone has to take her seriously."

"I certainly do," Scarlet agreed.

Tessa blinked. This was all just guesswork. There

wasn't one shred of real evidence against Lady Stella. But looking at the other girls' faces, she could tell some were wondering: was their beloved headmistress out to get them?

CHAPTER
5

"So what do you think?"

Tessa and Gemma were strolling through the Ozzie-fruit Orchard arm in arm, in the usual Starling fashion. It had been an uneventful day for Tessa; she hadn't once been late to class, and she'd been fully prepared for each. She'd even gone to the library to star apologize to Lady Floridia about missing independent study.

Now it was just after dinner at lightfall. Gemma had been chattering about going home for the Time of Lumiere and how they would spend their time: grooming the galliopes; taking care of the chickadoodles, the small winged creatures that couldn't fly; coaxing the fruit to grow.

But Tessa was wondering exactly what her sister

thought about the Lady Stella accusations. Earlier she'd just assumed that Gemma agreed with her that Lady Stella was innocent. But something about Gemma's expression in the Lightning Lounge made her want to find out for sure.

"I'm confused," Gemma answered. She stopped to twist an ozziefruit from its stem, then bit into the sweet indigo-colored fruit. Bright juice dribbled down her chin, and Tessa used wish energy to wipe it off. "I don't want to think Lady Stella is a bad Starling. But Cassie and Scarlet seem so sure. I mean, she did set up Ophelia to take Scarlet's place!"

"Well, I'm just as sure she's doing everything in her power to help us and Starland," said Tessa. "Maybe Ophelia made everything up about Lady Stella. Maybe she's star-crazed and just plain bitbatty."

Gemma took another bite of the ozziefruit. This time juice squirted down her dress. Tessa gazed at her sister and felt an urge to protect her. She seemed so young, so inexperienced. She was only a first year. How could she go on a mission when each one seemed more dangerous than the last?

"You know," Gemma said thoughtfully, as if reading Tessa's mind, "one of us could be chosen for the next mission."

Tessa nodded. At least she had already been to Wishworld, to help Sage with her mission. But that had been the very first one. It seemed like light-years had passed since that time.

Back then Tessa had thought the journey was an adventure—nothing more, nothing less. *If Sage doesn't manage to bring back wish energy, no big deal*, she'd thought. *There's always next time.* But things had gone wrong on most of the missions. And the trip itself could be dangerous. Just thinking of how Leona's shooting star had burned out made Tessa shiver. What if Vega hadn't been able to strap her onto her own star? She'd have been lost in space!

Tessa's Star-Zap went off suddenly, interrupting her thoughts. But it wasn't only her device buzzing; Gemma's was going off, too. And Tessa knew what that meant. They were getting the same holo-text from Lady Stella, telling the Star Darlings to report to her office immediately.

The sisters looked at each other. "The next mission!" they said in unison.

Lady Stella's office was so quiet you could hear a pin drop. Tessa and Gemma were the last to arrive. They took the only empty seats left: on either side of Lady Stella. Tessa glanced around the oval table.

Everyone wore serious expressions. The air seemed charged with excitement, and an undercurrent of anxiety swirled through the room. No one looked directly at Lady Stella.

The headmistress moved gracefully toward the window, her long gown sweeping the floor. As she had her back to the girls for a moment, they all exchanged nervous glances. When Lady Stella turned, Tessa was relieved to see her expression was as calm as ever.

"Star greetings," Lady Stella said warmly, letting her eyes linger on each girl for a moment. When she gazed at Tessa, Tessa felt her nervousness disappear like a puff of smoke.

Cassie was next, and Lady Stella rested her gaze on her longer than the others. Tessa saw Cassie smile at the headmistress—an open, admiring smile. Even Scarlet was moved, pulling down the hood of her black sweatshirt to soak in more warmth.

Lady Stella finally spoke. "I must star apologize to all of you. I've been so busy lately that I haven't spent enough time with any of you."

The girls murmured their agreement. Cassie nodded eagerly. Tessa felt her shoulders relax. She hadn't even realized how tense she'd been, worrying about Lady Stella and how the other Star Darlings felt about her. But now she felt so much brighter. She began to hope the next mission would be hers.

"Now let us see the new Wish Orb," Lady Stella said.

Linking arms and talking softly to one another, the group headed through the secret door, down the ladder, and into the dimly lit tunnels.

When they passed the spot where the bitbat had hung from Tessa's finger, she exchanged looks with Scarlet. There was nothing going on in those caves; no clues pointed to Lady Stella. Clearly the headmistress had nothing to hide.

The group reached the Wish Cavern. Tessa blinked in the bright sunlight, once again wondering how the sun could shine so far underground. The glittering waterfall cascaded to the ground like a moonium sparkle showers, and the grass felt as soft as a cloud beneath her feet. She sighed happily.

There was no evil plot spearheaded by Lady Stella, Tessa was sure of it. Maybe there wasn't a plot at all, just a random mix of mishaps. Tessa felt more relaxed than she had in a double starweek. It was the perfect frame of mind for a trip to Wishworld.

Only four girls had yet to go on a mission. Behind

her back, Tessa counted on her fingers: "Me, Gemma, Clover, and Adora. One of us will be chosen."

The girls grouped around the lush green platform and waited. Tessa squeezed between Gemma and Clover and took their hands. Then she leaned across Gemma to nod at Adora. All four girls leaned forward eagerly, hoping to see the Wish Orb as quickly as possible.

"Now," said Lady Stella, and the platform noiselessly parted. Four delicate Wish Orbs floated lazily into the air. *Four!*

"Are we all going?" asked Gemma breathlessly. "What kind of mission would be perfect for all four of us?"

But three of the orbs descended back into the platform as quietly as they had risen. "Guess not," said Gemma, sounding half glad, half disappointed. Tessa gave her a small smile; it would have been starmazing to go together.

The remaining Wish Orb swung this way and that in an almost hypnotic manner. Tessa followed the motion and, with every arc, felt her sleepy mind wander a bit farther. If only she'd eaten a bigger dinner, she would be wide-awake and ready for whatever the future might hold. She should have had another serving of noddlenoodle soup or more glorange juice or—

Suddenly, Clover elbowed her in the side. "Oh!" said Tessa. The Wish Orb had stopped right in front of her. She held out her hand, and the pulsing ball of energy settled gracefully in her palm.

"The orb has chosen," Lady Stella said, smiling. "As soon as you're ready, Tessa, you may leave."

Tessa grinned. "I can be ready in two shakes of a glion's tail."

"I do believe you can," said Lady Stella. "But I meant you can leave as soon as you're ready in the morning. You'll need a good starnight's rest."

CHAPTER
6

It was just as well Tessa hadn't hurried to Wishworld right after the orb had chosen. She hadn't realized just how much she had to do. First she needed to select a Wishling outfit. Something that would be comfortable and rugged, she thought, in case she wound up doing something outdoorsy like she hoped. After a star-hour or so, she settled on cropped jeans that had a hint of green in the blue material and a tailored button-down shirt with sleeves that could be rolled up easily.

Next she called Jewel to come out and play. She needed to say good-bye. The young galliope—even in virtual form—seemed to have grown in just that day. How big would she be when Tessa came back from her mission? "I'll be away," she told Jewel, "but I'll be think-ing of you."

In fact, Tessa would be more than "away." She'd be mooniums of floozels away. Did Jewel understand? And would she miss Tessa, too?

Quickly, Tessa holo-called Gemma. "Can you keep Jewel company while I'm gone?" she asked as Gemma's image hovered in front of her.

"Of course," Gemma said. "It will make me feel bet-ter, too."

Tessa gulped. She'd gotten used to seeing her sister every starday. It made being away from her parents and the farm much easier. "I'll be back before you know it," she said.

"In time for dinner?" Gemma asked teasingly.

"Oh my stars!" said Tessa. "You just gave me a bril-liant idea. Gotta go! I have hydrongs of things to do!"

Early the next morning, Tessa was finally ready and, she feared, late for her mission. She rushed around on the Cosmic Transporter, juggling boxes and containers and skirting students. The packages were piled so high she could barely see.

"Star excuse me," she said again and again, bumping into girls with every step.

Right in front of Halo Hall, she pressed past Vivica and Violetta.

Vivica snickered to Violetta. "What would happen if I 'accidentally' bumped into her right now?"

Tessa concentrated, using her wish energy manipulation to hold everything together. And she didn't bother to star apologize when she accidentally stepped on Vivica's foot.

Finally, she reached the Flash Vertical Mover, and she used her nose to press the button.

When she got to the top, the door whooshed open. Tessa, peering over her packages, saw everyone else already waiting on the deck that stood high above Starland.

"What on Starland are you carrying?" Sage asked as the Star Darlings crowded around, excited.

"Just some provisions." Tessa dropped everything at her feet and felt her shimmer flare in her embarrassment. She hadn't realized anyone would think it was strange. Gemma rooted through the pile.

"Astromuffins," she called out. "Garble greens and jujufruits. Star sandwiches with glimmer butter. Jujufruit tarts." She stopped to count. "A baker's glowzen of them!" She grinned at her sister. "What *didn't* you bring, Tessa?"

"I didn't have time for breakfast," Tessa said a little defensively. "And what if I don't like the food on Wishworld? I want to be prepared."

"Preparation is key to a successful mission," Lady Stella said, joining the group, her eyes twinkling. Then a serious look crossed her face. "Are you prepared, Tessa?"

Tessa had gone over everything again and again; she knew the importance of the mission and could rattle off tasks in her sleep.

Find her Wisher. Figure out the wish. Keep an eye on the Countdown Clock and monitor her energy levels. Recite her Mirror Mantra—the special phrase that would bring her glimmer back—when she needed a boost. And figure out her special talent as soon as possible. That would surely help her succeed.

Tessa touched her Wish Pendant, a silvery star brooch pinned to her collar. "Yes, Lady Stella," she answered.

"Now we will just wait for Lady Cordial to bring your backpack so you can take your provisions. And the wranglers will capture you a star." Lady Stella moved toward the Flash Vertical Mover to wait for Lady Cordial. As soon as she left the group, the mood changed.

A moogle before, Tessa noted, the girls had been

excited for her, same as they'd been for the other missions. But now they wore worried expressions.

Cassie leaned in close to Tessa. "Are you sure you're okay?" she asked anxiously. "I really don't know what to think! If Lady Stella is working against us, anything could happen."

Tessa *had* been fine. Why did Cassie have to go and say something?

Scarlet edged over, and Tessa found herself backing away. She didn't want to feel any more negative energy, not right before she left for Wishworld.

"Don't say a word, Scarlet," she commanded.

Scarlet nodded mutely, then reached over to hug Tessa tight. Tessa looked at her in amazement.

Then she gazed at Gemma and all the Star Darlings. Suddenly, she didn't want to go. "Don't worry about Jewel!" Gemma said, squeezing her hand.

"Or anything here." Cassie forced a smile. "Just have a starmendous mission."

"Stars crossed, I will," Tessa said. She tamped down her apprehension, once again visualizing Professor Margaret Dumarre's garden.

"S-s-s-star greetings," Lady Cordial stuttered, hurrying up to her, her purple hair escaping from her bun. "I have your backpack and keychain, Tessa."

"Star salutations," Tessa said, reaching to steady Lady Cordial before she tripped over a container of Sparkle-O's. Her heart went out to the older Starling. Standing next to regal Lady Stella, Lady Cordial seemed even smaller and stouter than usual. Tessa took the backpack, smiling, then quickly packed her supplies.

By then, the Star Wranglers had caught a star. After one last hug from Gemma, Tessa was ready to go. She made sure her backpack was secure and her Star-Zap was within easy reach. Cassie nodded her approval.

"Good luck St-st-starling!" called Lady Cordial. "This energy crisis isn't going to fix itself!" Then the head of admissions looked stricken and slapped her hand over her mouth. Lady Stella turned to her, her face twisted in shock. Had Tessa heard correctly? The other Star Darlings were staring at the two women, looking very confused indeed. And that's when the wranglers released Tessa's star into the heavens. She would have to put this possible new information out of her mind and concentrate on her mission. Still, it wasn't going to be easy.

Lights and shapes streaked past, a starmazing mix of heavenly bodies, bright flashes, and colorful beams. Tessa twisted her head this way and that, taking in each new sight, until her Star-Zap buzzed, signaling her final descent.

This was it. She recited the wish poem to change her appearance, her shimmer fading to a dull Wishling shade. Next she switched clothes and, an instant later, tumbled lightly to the ground.

"Oh my stars!" Tessa had landed on her back and was staring directly at the Wishworld sun. It seemed a bit dimmer than the suns of Starland but still impressive, she thought. She sat up, looked around, and gasped.

Farm fields stretched in front of her for what seemed like floozels, with neat rows of crops that resembled lighttuce and sunbeans. She saw a barn with a galliope-like creature just coming out of its red doors.

Maybe her Wisher was on that very farm!

"Let's move the billboard to the corner for now," she heard a male Wishling shout. "It will go on top of this building. But it needs to be out of the way during rush hour."

A truck engine revved, and the entire scene moved, revealing crowds of Wishlings hurrying along a city street behind it.

The farm was just a painting, a giant sign placed on top of a flatbed truck. Now she noticed there was even writing on it: VISIT THE U-PICK FARM, WHERE U HAVE FUN!

Tessa sprang to her feet. She was really on a street corner, not a farm. People rushed around her, not giving her a second glance. Most Wishlings wore jackets that matched their pants and skirts—either dark blue or black. Tessa was pleased to see her button-down shirt fit right in.

"Big meeting," one Wishling was saying into her cell phone. Tessa couldn't help staring. The phone looked like an early Star-Zap knockoff, but much more primitive. "Today was the worst day to oversleep," the Wishling went on. "Got to go. I'm late."

Everyone seemed to be heading toward a cluster of tall office buildings. There wasn't a young Wishling in sight, and Tessa highly doubted her Wisher was one of the office workers—"busy-ness people," Professor Margaret Dumarre had called them. And Tessa agreed; they all looked very busy and harried.

Feeling uncomfortable, Tessa wondered why she had been chosen for that mission. She was definitely out of her element. There were concrete sidewalks, there were hardly any trees, and she was about as far from a farm as a Starling could get—at least thirty miles away, according to the billboard. Whatever that meant!

Somewhere, a bell rang nine times, and everyone walked even faster. Then, like magic, the street emptied. The only people left were Tessa and the two billboard workers.

Tessa glanced around and noticed a street sign: COMMERCE STREET. Of course! Tessa almost laughed at herself. Distracted by all the hustle and bustle, she'd forgotten how simple locating her Wisher could be. All she had to do was check her Star-Zap for directions.

Following the route on the screen map, Tessa took the next left, walked two more blocks, and found herself on a quiet street. She walked toward a small brick building set back from the sidewalk. It looked a bit like the school buildings she'd seen through a Wishworld Surveillance Deck telescope. But this wasn't a school. A sign in the front yard read HILLSBORO ANIMAL SHELTER.

Tessa's heart skipped a beat. "'Animal,'" she read out loud, just to make sure. This might be even better than a farm! A wide smile spread across her face.

She knew the word *animal* meant a creature of some sort, hopefully friendly, like all the creatures on Starland. And *shelter* meant to protect. Animal shelter. It was an awfully big place to protect just one creature, she thought, even if it was the smallest building she'd seen so far.

But maybe the animal was huge! As big as a house! She'd read about one creature called a smellephant, so named because of its long, stretched-out nose, which could bend and curve and even pick up objects!

She paused. Maybe the creature was dangerous. The word *shelter* might mean protection *from*, not *for*, an animal. The building could provide a safe place for Wishlings.

Tessa glanced anxiously down the street. She willed herself to think positive thoughts. Once again, she called up the garden vision, and she added a few glober-beems for good measure. Her heartbeat slowed. She felt calmer.

Of course there were no dangerous animals there. Tessa was being star-crazed. She was in a small city, after all. There wouldn't be wild animals roaming the streets. Even in Starland City, you wouldn't find a glion or twinkelope wandering along the transporters.

Feeling better, Tessa walked up the building's path and stopped at the double glass doors. She tried peering in but couldn't make out much. So, taking a deep breath, she stepped inside and entered a lobby with a desk facing the entrance. There wasn't a creature in sight—or a Wishling, for that matter.

Tessa wandered to a wall covered with flat, unmoving pictures. Wishling photographs, she knew.

The photos featured Wishling creatures, some cuddling with children, some with adults, all adorable—and none as big as a house. In fact, most of them were quite small.

Tessa had taken every Wishling creature class she could back home—and had gotten an I in every one—so she was familiar with many of the animals. But they looked different here than in holo–artist renderings—and much clearer than from the Wishworld Surveillance Deck.

Her heart expanded as she looked at the animals, probably all in need, she realized. Cats and dogs, and others she didn't recognize.

One was a long, sleek creature that looked like a striped tube. It had no legs, and its head was part of its body. Tessa shivered.

But right next to that creature was a picture of a tiny, adorable animal, a ball of fur with big round cheeks and a small nose, running on some sort of wheel.

Next to the picture wall was a table piled high with sale items labeled DOGGY TREATS and CAT TOYS. To the side stood a big jar, filled with flat round silver objects.

Tessa read the sign on it: DONATIONS APPRECIATED. ALL PROCEEDS BENEFIT THE SHELTER.

Just then a woman walked briskly into the lobby from a hallway off to the side. She bent over the desk, flipping open a large book. *The book is made from paper!* Tessa thought excitedly.

"May I help you, dear?" the woman asked Tessa. She had short wavy gray hair, and when she smiled at Tessa, her eyes crinkled in a friendly way.

"Um." The woman had called her *deer*. Did she actually think Tessa was a Wishling creature that lived in the woods? Confused, Tessa just stood there for a moment. The woman gazed at her patiently, and finally, Tessa stepped closer.

The woman nodded encouragingly. "Our receptionist isn't here," she explained. "But you must be one of the students who are volunteering this summer. Since this is the first week of our program, we haven't figured out schedules or responsibilities yet."

She held out her hand. "My name is Penny Loar. I'm the director here. Please call me Penny. What is your name, dear? I'll check you off the list."

Tessa tapped the woman's fingers in what she hoped was the correct Wishling way. *Student volunteer,* she thought quickly. *Summer program.*

Summer was a season, similar to the Time of Lumiere, the warmest part of the staryear. Did Wishlings have a school break then? And had lots signed up to help at the shelter? It sounded like it, she decided. So this was definitely the place she'd meet her Wisher. Plus she was talking to the director, the head of the program. That was a stroke of luck.

Tessa smiled at Penny. She concentrated hard, blocking out all distracting thoughts, and said, "My name is Tessa. I did sign up to volunteer. I'm not on the list. But it doesn't matter."

Penny sniffed the air. A dreamy expression crossed her face. "Your name is Tessa," she repeated. "It doesn't matter that you're not on the list." She scribbled in the book, then looked up.

"Do you smell that, too?" she asked Tessa. "Someone nearby must be baking my favorite pastry, raisin cinnamon buns. I had one every morning for breakfast growing up."

Tessa grinned. The mind-control trick really was starmazing! Too bad it only worked on adults.

"I'm so sorry I'm late, Penny!" another woman said, hurrying into the lobby. She pinned a name tag—DONNA—onto her shirt, also button-down, Tessa noted. "I can take over now."

"That's okay," said Penny. "This is Tessa, one of our summer volunteers. I'll take her in the back and get her started."

Tessa still wasn't entirely sure what the shelter did, but it looked like she had a job!

CHAPTER
7

Penny was leading Tessa down a long hall, explaining what the shelter did.

"Most of our animals are strays, lost or abandoned pets people find in the streets. Sometimes owners bring them in, too, if they're moving to a place that doesn't allow animals, or they feel they can't care for them anymore. Here we give animals medical care, clean and feed them, and try to exercise them as much as possible. And of course, we try to find them homes!"

Tessa held in a gasp. Wishling creatures could be lost or abandoned—things that never really happened on Starland. Now she understood what the shelter was. It was there to help any local animal in trouble.

Penny stepped into a small room filled floor to ceiling with gray metal cabinets. "We're changing over to a computerized system for our files," she told Tessa, "but we're still holding on to our paper records, just in case there's a problem."

Paper again! And there must be hydrongs of sheets in those drawers. But why all the paper records? Hadn't she learned in Wishling History that records had something to do with music? Were those files filled with songs?

Tessa shook her head to clear it. Music probably had nothing to do with her mission. She needed to focus on the here and now. So she just nodded knowingly.

"Anyway, I'm sure you want to see the animals," Penny said. "After all, that's why you're here! Let's start with the dogs."

She took Tessa through another door, marked DOGGY DAY CARE. Tessa stepped into the huge space and tried to take everything in.

First there was the noise. Yips, yaps, and barks echoed loudly. Along one wall, little rooms stood side by side in a row. Each one had a gate in front, like a half door. And behind each gate, a dog stood, jumped, paced, or slept.

It was a little disturbing to see animals cooped up

like that, but Tessa wasn't really shocked. She'd heard about zoos and aquariums, and she supposed this was for the animals' own good, too. It would be pandemonium to let all those animals roam loose. Besides, the spaces were good-sized, neat, and clean, and every dog had a little bed, a food dish, and a water bowl.

"Each dog has its own kennel," Penny said. "The kennels have swinging doors that open to the outside, with separate yards."

"R-r-r-r-fffff!" A big sloppy-looking dog with floppy ears and curly hair rushed toward his door, barking loudly. Tessa bent over the gate to scratch him behind the ears.

"This is Tiny," Penny said with a laugh. "We name all the dogs that come in, if they don't have names already." She sighed. "Tiny has been with us about a year now. The big dogs have a tough time finding homes."

"You mean they can go out and look for houses, too?" Tessa asked, confused.

Penny laughed, as if she'd made a funny joke. "That would be something! Imagine if that was true. Instead of people coming here, looking at animals and picking one to take home, the animals did the choosing! Or bought their own houses!"

Penny explained further, and slowly Tessa was able

to piece together more about the shelter. As for Tiny, his family had brought him in because he barked and jumped on people, and they'd given up on training him. They just didn't want him around.

"How horrible!" said Tessa. She buried her face in Tiny's furry neck, trying to hide her tears.

Next Penny showed her the outside kennel yards, where dogs chewed on bones or nosed balls. Some puppies were grouped together. *They're the cutest things ever,* Tessa thought. They had paws that looked too big for their bodies and large soulful eyes.

Penny pointed out the dog run, a giant fenced-in area where dogs raced around, playing, while a volunteer sat at a nearby picnic table, overseeing them.

"The dogs come out here at least twice a day," Penny went on. "But we also walk them, so hopefully they do their business outside." She smiled at Tessa. "That should make it easier to clean the kennels. But you'll find out about that later."

Tessa frowned. What did *do their business* mean?

All in all, Tessa didn't like the sound of it. What exactly would she be cleaning? Spilled food? Something else? But maybe she'd finish her mission before it came time for any tidying up. Discreetly, she checked

her Countdown Clock. Already a few Wishworld hours
had passed. And her Wisher still hadn't appeared. Tessa's
Wish Pendant hadn't so much as blinked, let alone
glowed brightly to signal her Wisher was near.

"Now for the cats," said Penny, opening a door
marked CAT CONDOS. Inside, large comfy cages housed
the creatures, some singly, some in groups. A few cats
were playing in the middle of the room, in a large open
area filled with toys.

One volunteer sat on the floor, playing with a
baby cat—a kitten, Tessa realized. The kitten had gray
and black stripes, a tiny pink nose, and ears that stood
straight up at attention.

The volunteer motioned for Tessa to come closer,
then scooped up the small creature for Tessa to hold.
The kitten nestled against her chest and purred. Tessa's
heart flipped; she wanted to take the creature home with
her right that starsec.

She imagined the kitten going to class with her,
watching her bake, and then going to the farm on school
breaks and playing with Jewel. Of course, it could never
happen. But at that moment, Tessa wished for it.

"I like you," a soft voice murmured. Tessa turned to
Penny and said, "I like you, too."

Penny smiled a little uncertainly, as if she didn't know why Tessa had blurted that out. "That's good," she said, "since we'll be working together."

Reluctantly, Tessa put the kitten down so Penny could show her more: visiting rooms for prospective owners, examination rooms, grooming rooms, and a storage room filled with bags and bags of animal food. Last, Penny showed her the room that housed a few snakes—those slippery creatures without legs—and some hamsters, the animal Tessa had seen pictured on a wheel. One hamster's expression reminded Tessa of a glowfur's, so she asked, "How many songs does she know?"

Once again, Penny gave her a funny look. Then she said, "I don't believe she knows any!"

There was also one adorable black creature with a white stripe down his back. Penny said most of the staff stayed away from him, and she added something about a bad odor, but Tessa wasn't really listening. She was still straining to hear the hamster, just in case she started to sing.

"Okay, that's the tour," Penny announced, taking Tessa back to the dog room. "How long will you be stay-ing today?"

Tessa almost said, *Until I meet my Wisher and help*

grant her wish. But she stopped herself just in time. "As long as you need me."

"Good. Mostly you'll shadow a staff member or volunteer to learn how things work around here. But right now, I think Tiny needs a walk." She pulled down a long strap from a peg. "This is Tiny's leash. Just attach it to his collar."

A leash? A collar? Starland creatures had neither of those. Tessa looked at Penny helplessly.

"I'll show you," Penny said, "because it can be tricky getting it on, and getting Tiny out safely. You don't want him taking off."

Taking off? Like a shooting star? Now Tessa was really confused. She pictured wings unfolding from under Tiny's fur. "You mean Tiny can fly?"

Penny laughed. "He sure can. He runs so fast it is just like flying! But seriously, you need to be careful he doesn't run away."

Penny demonstrated how to lean over and snap on the leash before she opened the gate. Tessa immediately reached down to pet Tiny. She looked into his big brown eyes and felt a spark of recognition, a connection like they'd known each other for staryears.

"Hi," said a voice.

Tessa looked around. It was a deep male voice, and only Penny was standing nearby.

"I said hello. Are you going to walk me? I love walks. I love to sniff the air. I love to chase squirrels."

What? Was that Tiny talking? And what in the stars was a squirrel?

Tiny tilted his head, as if expecting answers, and it hit Tessa like a lightning bolt: she could understand his thoughts—the same way she had earlier with the kitten, she now realized. Penny hadn't said she liked her! It had been the tiny adorable creature. That must be Tessa's special talent—knowing animals' thoughts!

She looked at the other dogs but couldn't pick up any voices. Maybe she needed to feel a special closeness.

Meanwhile, Penny was still talking, unaware of what had just happened. "So stay away from busy sidewalks and the highway out back. But everywhere else is fine."

Tessa didn't want to ask what a highway was. She felt embarrassed enough, having blurted out that she liked Penny without the Wishling's saying she liked Tessa first!

Anyway, a highway was probably a street of some sort, Tessa figured. But how high did it reach? She grew a little excited, imagining walking Tiny up among the stars, even though Penny had said to stay away from it.

Now Penny was holding out the leash. As soon as

Tessa took it, Tiny raced out of the kennel, then straight out a side door, taking Tessa with him.

At least Tiny knows where he's going, Tessa thought as she tried to keep her balance. He was pulling her along, barking happily, and Tessa heard him thinking, *Good girl, you can do it. Just keep running!* He was encouraging her, almost as if she was his pet!

Together, they ran through a small wooded area behind the shelter, then right by a busy road, where cars zipped along as fast as comets.

Highway, highway! Tiny thought. *I love to chase cars!*

Tessa struggled to keep him under control. "Slow down, Tiny!" she shouted. Really, they should call the road a fastway, not a highway. She hoped Tiny wouldn't jump the guardrail on the side.

"Stop!" Tessa pleaded, and luckily, Tiny listened, settling down to stay by Tessa's heels. Together they watched the cars for a bit—really rather unpleasant, Tessa thought. All that noise and smoky exhaust. How did Wishlings stand it? Of course, there weren't any homes nearby, so maybe they didn't like it, either!

After a while, Tiny led her back through the woods and into the shelter. Inside, a staff member showed Tessa how to fill water bowls and food dishes and how to clean out the kennels while the dogs were outside.

Cleaning wasn't as bad as Tessa had feared. She put on protective gloves and used something called a pooper-scooper. But most everything had already been funneled down the sloping ground into a drain. All she really had to do was spray a soapy mixture all around the kennel and hose down the floor.

"Nice work," said Penny, passing by.

Tessa felt as pleased as if she'd earned all Is.

That afternoon, Tessa helped a couple choose a puppy to take home and gave two dogs baths. That wasn't fun at all. She almost suggested the dogs take sparkle showers instead. They were so resistant to getting into the big tub! Luckily, she remembered Wishlings didn't even have sparkle showers.

Meanwhile, a constant stream of visitors came into and went out of the shelter. But so far her Wisher was nowhere to be seen.

After the doggy baths, Penny asked Tessa to take some photos. Tessa held the camera gingerly as she walked through the cats' play area. How did it work, exactly? Starland's glamera was a small egg-shaped device you could hold in your palm. But this was a big bulky object that you strapped around your neck like some kind of fashion accessory.

Play with me! the striped kitten squeaked to her. So Tessa convinced a volunteer to take photos of her and the kitten together.

Later Tessa organized the sales table in the lobby with Penny. She was thinking that things on Wishworld were similar to Starland yet so different at the same time, when a big drop of water fell—*splat*—on her head. She moved a few star inches to her left, and more drops plopped around her.

"What's that?" she asked, wondering if somebody else had had the idea of showering the animals and this was some sort of a test run.

Penny sighed, reaching for buckets they kept under the front desk. "Remember it rained yesterday?"

The starday had been glowrious on Starland, but Tessa nodded.

"Whenever it rains, our roof starts leaking sometime the next day. The roof is so old it really needs to be replaced, or at least repaired. But we're low on funds as it is. We have just enough money to cover basic care of our animals. So that's on hold." She smiled at Tessa. "Thank goodness we have volunteers to help. I can't tell you how grateful I am that you worked all day. But we're closing up shop now."

Tessa could see the sunlight dimming outside. The whole Wishworld day had passed, and she hadn't even caught a glimpse of her Wisher.

"Is it okay if I come back tomorrow?" she asked Penny.

"Of course. But we should really nail down your schedule for the rest of the summer." Penny took out the volunteer book and looked at Tessa expectantly.

Oh, no, not again! Tessa looked into Penny's eyes and said, "You do not need my schedule."

Penny closed the book. "I do not need your schedule." She shook her head. "And there's that raisin cinnamon smell again. I think I'll stop off at the bakery on my way home."

CHAPTER
8

That night, Tessa unfolded her star tent and pitched it in the dog run, careful to find a clean, clear spot. The tent popped up easily, complete with everything Tessa could want—including a portable micro-zap.

Tessa knew the tent was invisible to Wishling eyes. But she wondered briefly if animals could spot it. Either way, she needed to be up and out before anyone came to the shelter in the morning. Good thing the bells she'd heard chiming when she first arrived continued to ring every hour on the hour. That was one way to keep track of Wishworld time.

Tessa eyed her Countdown Clock uneasily. She probably had two to three Wishworld days left, with so much still to do! But it wouldn't help to worry or let her mind wander back to problems on Starland.

Instead, she smoothed the deep plush rug that stretched across the floor. She plumped her luxurious pillows, chosen specially for the trip, and sank into her bed, between cool smooth sheets. There. It was almost like being home. She stretched, reaching for warmed-up tarts and sandwiches on the nightstand.

Now what? Tessa didn't feel tired at all! So she fiddled around with her Star-Zap and found a Wishling video called *Middle School Musical 2*. It followed students throughout a day at school. Tessa made a note in her Cyber Journal especially for Leona: *Sometimes Wishlings break out in song to express their feelings—even if glowfur-like creatures don't!*

Tessa must have been more tired than she realized. The next thing she knew, the bell sounded nine times. *Starf!* She'd better hurry. The shelter would open any starmin. As quickly as she could, she packed her things and rushed to the front entrance.

A Wishling girl was walking down the path just ahead. The girl had straight reddish hair, tied back in a short bobbing ponytail. If Tessa squinted, the red hair looked orange and she looked just like Gemma! Tessa felt a pang. *But wait*, she thought. Maybe the pang was really a tingle, a clue that her Wisher was nearby. She looked down at her brooch. Sure enough, Tessa's Wish Pendant was glowing brightly. This girl was her Wisher!

"Hey!" Tessa said, running a bit to catch up.

The girl stopped, then grinned. "Hey, yourself! Are you a new volunteer with the summer program? I've been volunteering here all year, so if you want, I can show you around. Do you love animals, too? I have a dog named Fiona, but I love all the animals here."

Did the girl talk as much as Gemma, too? That was starmendously perfect.

"My name is Tessa," said Tessa, smiling happily. "I—I mean, my family and I—just moved to Hillsboro. Otherwise I would have been working here all year!"

"I'm Lizzie," said the girl. Tessa thought she'd ask questions about Tessa's family, or where she lived, or where she was going to school. She had already prepared some answers. Instead, a shadow crossed Lizzie's face and she fell silent.

Together, the girls walked into the shelter and said good morning to Donna and Penny. Tessa heard barks and meows and some random thoughts.

I'm hungry!

That's my catnip!

Hope my walker comes soon!

But she tried to shut them out.

No distractions, she told herself firmly. *Now is the time to concentrate on Lizzie.*

First order of business: figuring out her wish. Tessa had to stick close to her, get her talking again.

"I'm supposed to be shadowing someone this morning, to learn more," Tessa said to Lizzie. "Can you be my person?"

"Sure!" Lizzie brightened. "I can teach you everything I know. It's good, really, because"—there was that shadow again—"today is my last day, and I'll feel better knowing you're here."

Before Tessa could ask a question or get more information, Lizzie turned away. "I usually feed the dogs their breakfast first thing."

"Okay," said Tessa, following Lizzie to the storage room, where they filled bowl after bowl. Lizzie would only be there that day! Tessa really had to act quickly.

When Tessa brought Tiny a bowl, he threw his body against the gate and wagged his tail harder than any other dog.

"Wow, that's some greeting," said Lizzie. "Tiny is usually very particular, so you must have a way with animals."

"I hope so," Tessa said with a laugh. "We used to live

on a farm." She slipped inside the kennel, careful to close the door quickly. Tiny jumped all around her, and it was all Tessa could do to put down the bowl without spilling any food.

Tiny swung his head back and forth, looking at the bowl, then Tessa. Clearly, he was torn. But in the end, food won. As he slurped his breakfast, Tessa quietly edged outside to rejoin Lizzie.

"You must miss the farm terribly," Lizzie said. "Just like I'm going to miss this shelter. We're moving away, too, in just a few days. That's why I won't be working here anymore."

Lizzie was moving away. This was important information. Maybe her wish had something to do with that.

Lizzie carried a bowl to the kennel next door. A little black-and-white dog backed into a corner and looked at her warily. "Here, Trixie," Lizzie called softly. The dog was so thin Tessa could see her ribs. She couldn't tell what Trixie was thinking at all.

"Come on, girl," Lizzie said encouragingly. "Come eat." She put down the bowl, then slowly pushed it closer. Trixie didn't move. Lizzie moved it a little closer, then closer still.

Tessa held her breath. Finally, Trixie bent her head over the bowl and began to nibble.

For a long moment, Lizzie stayed as still as a statue. Finally, she backed out of the kennel, barely making a sound. "I'll give her some space now. But I think we just made some progress. Yesterday she wouldn't eat at all."

"You really know what to do," Tessa said admiringly.

"Well, I've worked at a bunch of different shelters. My parents are both in the military, and they're always getting different assignments. We've lived all over the world, some places less than a year. Volunteering with animals makes me feel better each time we have to move." She took a breath.

That was Lizzie's longest speech since her hello, Tessa realized. She hoped Lizzie didn't regret telling her so much.

"Anyway, I'm here all day today," Lizzie added. "How about you?"

That scheduling question again! "I don't know. . . ." Tessa snuck a peek at the Countdown Clock in case anything had changed since she last checked.

"Oh, you have to call home and check?" Lizzie asked, misunderstanding.

"Uh, yes," said Tessa. "But I'm sure it will be fine." She swiped her Star-Zap a few times and got ready to have a pretend conversation. But a voice with a much different accent from Lizzie's answered.

"This is Regina Barnes at the London office of Barnes, Barnes, and Barnes. How may I help you?" The woman's voice was loud enough for Lizzie to hear.

"Oops! Wrong number!" Tessa hung up. "I'll just text later."

Lizzie looked at her sympathetically. "I know it's hard getting used to different home numbers—and everything else."

"It is hard!" said Tessa. "I can't believe I just called London instead of Hillsboro!" Tessa acted like she knew all about London. But for all she really knew, it could be the next town over.

"We actually lived in London for a while," said Lizzie. "And it wasn't so bad being out of the country. I had a great friend named Nola who lived next door. We still keep in touch." She smiled at Tessa. "I try to stay friends with people I like. You should give me your contact info before we say good-bye."

"Sure," said Tessa. If only she and Lizzie really could stay in touch. *Wouldn't that be starmazing?* she thought. Her mind wandered to scenes in which she and Lizzie were both grown-up, traveling back and forth . . . meeting each other's families . . . going to each other's weddings.

"Tessa?" said Lizzie. "Are you all right? You have a funny expression on your face."

"I'm fine," Tessa said firmly, blinking her eyes to shake away the thoughts. She *was* fine, as long as she kept her mind on the mission. No distractions. "What should we do next?"

A few starmins later, they were settled in a quiet area of the cat condos room, holding miniature baby bottles to feed milk to the kittens.

Me! Me! Tessa heard the thoughts of the kitten she'd cuddled the day before coming from one of the cages. Gently, she scooped her out from a pile of snuggling cats. "I'll call you Snuggles!" she said.

Lizzie showed her how to hold Snuggles in the crook of one arm and tip the tiny bottle by her mouth so she would start to drink. Then she took her own kitten and sat next to Tessa.

Tessa smiled as Snuggles drank. *Mmmmm*, the tiny creature thought. Tessa could have sat there all day, holding and looking at Snuggles. But she reminded herself that she was on Wishworld for a reason. She had to find out Lizzie's wish.

"So," she said softly, trying not to disturb Snuggles, "it must be really hard moving around so much."

For Tessa herself, it would be near impossible to leave the farm. Her family had owned the land for generations.

Every starnight, she'd look up at the sky, find her great-grandparents' and her great-great-grandparents' stars twinkling down at her, and know they were pleased.

Tessa knew that after she graduated and finished her Wishworld duties, she'd go back to Solar Springs. She wasn't so sure about Gemma, who liked to be more in the center of things. But at least Gemma would always have a place to call home.

"Do you have sisters or brothers? Or both?" Tessa asked Lizzie.

Lizzie shook her head. "It's just my parents and me—and my dog, Fiona, of course." She smiled. "She's almost like a sister! We've basically grown up together. I don't remember a time she wasn't with us."

Tessa smiled back. That was nice, and it sounded like Lizzie had a strong family. But maybe she wanted roots, just one place to call home.

Maybe Lizzie's wish was to stay right there in Hillsboro.

"Do you wish you weren't moving?"

Lizzie shrugged. "No, I'm really okay with it. And it's necessary for my family. It's all part of my parents' jobs."

Tessa mentally crossed that off the wish list.

Lizzie looked at Tessa a little anxiously. "Don't get me wrong. Hillsboro is a great place. I'm sure you'll like it here. I've made a ton of friends."

"Oh!" Tessa straightened. Maybe the wish had to do with friendship.

Snuggles looked at her questioningly, so Tessa relaxed a bit and waited for the kitten to get comfortable.

"I bet you wish you could make tons of friends at your new school."

"I think I will. Making friends has always been pretty easy for me. You know," Lizzie said with a laugh. "I've had lots of practice."

Okay, so making friends wasn't the wish, either.

"Would you want your friends to throw you a good-bye party?" Tessa asked.

"They already have," Lizzie told her, "the last day of school." She stood and carefully put her kitten back in the cage. "Let's walk some dogs now."

For the rest of the morning, Tessa and Lizzie worked together. They walked Tiny and a dog named Oliver. They watched over more dogs at the dog run and took some visitors around the shelter. Lizzie was welcoming and courteous to everyone, and Tessa could see she did indeed make friends quickly.

In fact, Tessa felt like she and Lizzie were becoming

friends. That was nice. But between taking care of the animals and talking, Tessa kept forgetting about her mission. So just to be on the safe side, she set her Star-Zap on reminder mode, to go off every Wishworld hour.

When it went off at lunchtime, Tessa asked, "Do you wish you were moving to a different place?"

"No," said Lizzie. "We're going to Australia, and I'm curious about it. I've never been there before."

When the alarm buzzed an hour after that, while they were cleaning litter boxes, Tessa asked, "Do you wish you could finish the summer program here?"

"Not really," Lizzie said. "Of course I'll miss the animals, but I'm planning to volunteer at an Australian shelter, too." She looked at Tessa curiously. "You sure like to ask a lot of questions."

Tessa blushed.

"Star apolo—I mean, I'm sorry if you think I'm a busybody. It's just time is running out . . . I mean, you'll be leaving soon and I have so many questions about moving and making friends."

The afternoon passed, with Tessa asking more questions and getting no real answers. At five o'clock Penny said, "That's it, girls. The shelter is closing."

Then she put her arm around Lizzie. "Thank you so much for all your help. Make sure you stay in touch. You have our shelter e-mail, my personal e-mail, and all our addresses?"

Lizzie nodded, a little teary. "My mom's outside waiting. I'd better go."

No! Tessa thought. *You can't leave.* But then she realized she had to go, too. Together, the two girls walked through the door. "Are you sure you can't come back tomorrow?" Tessa asked.

"Yes, I'm sure," Lizzie said. "There's too much to do. I have to run errands. Pack. We're leaving the day after." Then she smiled. "Hey, come home with me for dinner! And this way, you can keep asking me questions."

"That would be great!" said Tessa, pretending to text her mom as they stood outside. The sky was overcast, and the air felt damp and warm.

Down the path, Lizzie's mom was waiting in the car. "This is Tessa," Lizzie said. "She's new here, and I just invited her to dinner."

Lizzie's mom frowned. "Honey, our house is almost all packed up, and you need to take care of so many things!"

Tessa stepped closer to the car. Remembering how Wishling adults liked to be addressed, she said, "Hi, Mrs.—" Tessa paused, realizing she didn't even know Lizzie's last name.

"Bennett," said Lizzie.

"Mrs. Bennett," Tessa continued. "I can be a big help. I should come for dinner."

"You can be a big help," Mrs. Bennett said slowly. "You should come for dinner." She glanced across the street. "Is there a new bakery around here? I smell chocolate éclairs, just like I had growing up."

"That's great!" said Lizzie. "It will be nice to have company while I pack."

Tessa breathed a sigh of relief. At least now she would have more time with her Wisher. Still, she'd been on Wishworld two days already, and there was lots left to do. Besides figuring out the wish, she still had to help make it come true!

CHAPTER
9

Lizzie's house was bare yet full. All the furniture was pushed to the side, the tables cleared of any odds and ends and knickknacks. The walls and counters were bare, too. But boxes littered the floor, and Tessa had to move in a zigzag just to walk from room to room.

She was following Lizzie into the living room when she heard the *click-clack* of nails against the hardwood floor. Suddenly, a small shape hurled itself at Lizzie.

"Fiona!" cried Lizzie, squatting on the floor to hug the little dog close.

Tessa sat down next to her and oohed. "She's so tiny!"

"She's a miniature dachshund," Lizzie said.

"Bless you," said Tessa, thinking Lizzie had sneezed.

Tessa smiled, relieved she'd remembered the Wishworld response.

"No." Lizzie laughed. "She's a miniature dachshund! That's her breed!"

Tessa laughed, too, leaning closer to pat Fiona's tummy when she rolled over. The dog's whole body wriggled with joy.

The girls took Fiona for a walk, then packed Lizzie's books and games. "Let's leave the stuffed animals," Lizzie said. "I want to sleep with them tonight."

Mrs. Bennett, who had dropped off the girls and then gone to pick up Mr. Bennett and dinner, returned.

"I'm sorry you're not getting a home-cooked meal, but our kitchen is in boxes," Mr. Bennett said, carrying in drinks and paper cups. He was very tall, with the same reddish hair as Lizzie, and the same warm smile.

"No, no," said Tessa. "This is all fine." But she did feel a little disappointed. The kitchen was big and spacious, and for a starmin she daydreamed about learning to bake the Wishling way—right on Wishworld. But that would have to wait for another mission—if she ever completed this one!

"I just have sandwiches," Mrs. Bennett warned Tessa. "Nothing fancy. I hope that's okay."

Tessa took a big bite of one sandwich, which wasn't really a sandwich at all. It looked more like a long stuffed tube—a "wrap," she'd heard Mrs. Bennett call it before handing one to Lizzie. Specifically, a Caesar salad wrap.

Tessa had been afraid she'd actually have to make a grab for Lizzie's sandwich in order to eat. Why else would it be called a "seize her" salad? But it turned out there were enough sandwiches for everyone.

"This is delicious," Tessa told Mrs. Bennett enthusiastically.

Lizzie's mom beamed. "It is very nice to have you here, Tessa. Why don't you sleep over, too? It would be nice for Lizzie to have a friend close by. We all could use a little extra support right now." She reached out to squeeze Lizzie's hand.

"Moving isn't easy for any of us," Mr. Bennett added. "But these are the choices we've made, and I wouldn't want to do it with anyone other than you two."

Lizzie nodded seriously, squeezing her mom's hand back. Then she turned to Tessa. "Say yes!" she pleaded. "Stay over! Please!"

"Sure!" said Tessa, happy she didn't have to use her mind control power. That took energy, and to be honest, she was feeling a little tired. She knew exhaustion was a side effect of being on Wishworld too long without granting a wish.

Just before bedtime, Tessa excused herself to go to the bathroom. There she peered at her image in the mirror. A Tessa-like being, without the shine or sparkle and with dark circles under her eyes, gazed back at her. Clearly, it was time for her mantra. She needed more energy.

Still looking at her reflection, Tessa recited, "Let your heart lead the way." Immediately, she felt a lift.

In the mirror, the real, sparkly Tessa gazed back, making Tessa feel even better. Bit by bit, her shimmer faded. But the strength remained. She could do this! *Now, back to Lizzie*, she thought.

The girls talked long into the night. Tessa wasn't getting any closer to Lizzie's wish. Still, she felt optimistic. She felt sure she would find out the wish before the sun rose. But then she couldn't help it: stretched out in a sleeping bag on the floor, Tessa fell into a deep sleep. Lizzie was already snoring gently in another sleeping bag, Fiona by her side.

Boom! A crash of thunder sounded, waking both girls. For an instant, lightning lit the room as bright as daylight. Tessa could see Lizzie sitting up, holding a quivering Fiona.

"It's okay, girl," Tessa said, reaching to stroke Fiona's head. "It's over."

But another roll of thunder roared, followed by an even louder crack. Rain pounded the roof and lashed at the windows.

The room lit up again, and Tessa saw Lizzie brush a tear from her cheek.

"Don't cry, Lizzie," she said. "I know thunderstorms are scary. But it really will be over soon."

"No, it's not that." Lizzie carried Fiona with her to the windows, making sure they were all tightly closed.

"But you're upset," Tessa said. She looked at Lizzie's tear-streaked face, and her heart went out to the Wishling girl. "It must be the move, then," she said. "You really don't want to go, do you?"

"I shouldn't feel this way!" Lizzie said with a hiccup. "But you're right. I don't want to move."

She snuggled back into the sleeping bag with Fiona and turned to face Tessa. "I told you I was fine with it. But I was trying to convince myself! I kept saying, 'It's exciting . . . it's an adventure. . . .' But that's not how I feel at all."

She burrowed her nose into Fiona's soft neck. "I've moved so often I know I can handle it. I just don't want to."

"You can't help the way you feel," Tessa said encouragingly. This was it, she knew; she was getting close to the wish.

"It's hard always being the new kid. I always get lost. I have to figure out a new school. And if we're in a different country, there's strange money and food. And just when I start to feel comfortable, we have to get up and move again.

"I know I should be happy," Lizzie continued, as if the floodgates had opened on her feelings. "I mean, how many kids can say they've traveled from Alaska to Zimbabwe?"

Or from Starland to Wishworld, Tessa added to herself, realizing she was lucky, too. The difference was she could always go back.

"And I know my parents' work is important. I don't want them to worry about me. They have enough going on." She grabbed Tessa's hand. "I just wish I could find one good thing about it. Just one thing about the move that makes me happy."

Tessa had it! She had the wish!

Lizzie yawned. "I don't mean to burden you, Tessa. But I've been keeping it all inside for so long . . ." Her eyes began to close. "It will probably be fine. . . ." And she fell asleep.

Tessa, meanwhile, was still wide-awake. Lizzie's wish: figured out. Making Lizzie's wish come true? That was entirely different.

She had to find one good thing about Lizzie's move— just one. But it had to be important enough to outweigh all the drawbacks. And she had to get Lizzie to see it, too.

⭐

Both girls slept late the next morning. By the time they went downstairs, Lizzie's parents were already gone. "They left a note," Lizzie said. She read the message stuck to the refrigerator door. Then she groaned. "They left a to-do list, too." Quickly, she scanned the items. "It's so long!"

"I'm not going to the shelter today," Tessa said. "If you like, I can hang out with you and help."

Lizzie grinned. "That would be great. The first thing on the list is to go out for breakfast. So you can help me eat!"

Outside, the air had the clean, fresh smell that came

after a big storm, and sunshine dappled the sidewalk.

"Let's go into Hillsboro Square to my favorite diner," said Lizzie, linking arms with Tessa, just like a Starling would.

A diner! Tessa had been curious about diners ever since Piper had come back from her mission and reported that she'd worked in one.

They walked in the opposite direction of the shelter. After only a few blocks, they reached the square. Tessa gazed at the small shops and narrow streets. It was so different from the area with the big buildings near the animal shelter. People were strolling, taking their time. And there were more bicycles than cars.

The Square Diner was busy, but the girls took seats at the counter and were served quickly. Tessa followed Lizzie's lead and ordered the pancakes. They weren't much different from starcakes, she realized after eating a forkful. All her fears about strange Wishling food were definitely unfounded.

After they finished, Lizzie picked up a piece of paper the server had left by their plates. It was filled with scribbles and numbers in columns. "I'll pay the check," she said.

"Excuse me?" Tessa said, not understanding.

"No, I insist!" said Lizzie. She took out green slips of paper with men's faces in the middle and numbers in the corners.

This must be money! Tessa thought. She had only the vaguest idea of Wishworld economy. Turning away from Lizzie, Tessa noted in her Cyber Journal that it might be a good idea to have a Wishworld economics class. She added that geography would be helpful, too. All those Wishworld place names Lizzie had rattled off! It was all so confusing.

Just as Lizzie finished counting out the money, a man came over, wiping his hands on his apron. He whisked away the check and said, "Your breakfast is on me."

Tessa squinted up at the man's head. There was nothing on it, not even hair, let alone a batch of pancakes.

"You and your family have been wonderful customers all year long," he continued. "We'll miss you around here, Lizzie."

Next Lizzie took Tessa to the Hillsboro General Store. They bought heavy-duty tape, markers to label boxes, and some cleaning supplies. "Just one more thing and we're done," said Lizzie, checking the list. "Packing peanuts."

"Peanuts?" Tessa perked up. Wasn't that a tasty treat

she'd heard about during a Wishling Cuisine lesson? Of course, she knew many Wishlings had bad reactions to peanuts. What was the reaction called? Something that sounded like energy. But Tessa doubted a Starling would be affected.

When Lizzie passed her a bag, she opened it right up and popped a peanut into her mouth. Immediately, she spat it out. "That's horrible!" she exclaimed.

"Of course it is," Lizzie said. "It's Styrofoam."

Tessa had no idea where Styrofoam grew, but she certainly wouldn't recommend any Star Darling try it while on a mission.

They moved to the counter to pay, and the owner smiled sadly at Lizzie. "I hear you're leaving us," she said. "We're all going to miss you." She rang up Lizzie's purchases on a big machine. Then she said, "Wait right here!"

The owner hurried to something called the deli section and returned with a big bone. "For Fiona," she explained. "A good-bye gift."

All day, everywhere they went, it seemed, shop owners were wishing Lizzie well and sometimes throwing in a farewell present. People stopped her on the street to say good-bye.

Tessa thought it all would make Lizzie happy. *Could*

that be the one good thing? she wondered. Instead, Lizzie's eyes filled with tears again and again. Sometimes, Tessa supposed, acts of kindness could make you cry more than anything else.

By the time they got back to the house, the sun was setting. Tessa worried that Lizzie would send her home, since it was getting late. But instead, Lizzie asked for more help packing.

Together, Tessa and Lizzie poured the packing peanuts into half-filled boxes of vases and glass bowls so the fragile objects wouldn't break in the moving truck.

So that's what they're for, thought Tessa. "Hey," she shouted to Lizzie. "Try to catch this!" And she tossed a lighter-than-air peanut in Lizzie's direction.

Lizzie lunged for it but missed—by a floozel. Tessa laughed. Then Lizzie grabbed a handful and threw them at Tessa. "Peanut fight!" she cried. She giggled loudly and emptied an entire bag over Tessa's head.

Abruptly, Tessa stopped laughing.

"I'm sorry!" Lizzie said. "Did I go overboard with the packing peanuts?"

"Huh?" said Tessa. She was staring into space, confused.

"What's going on?"

"Shhh! Just give me a starmin." Tessa didn't bother to correct herself and say *minute*. She was too busy concentrating. Just before Lizzie had poured the peanuts, she'd picked up some sort of signal. It was a cry for help that sounded strangely like a bark. She was hearing other thoughts, too: a kitten mewling in panic, another dog shouting for someone, anyone, to get her.

"Tessa?"

Tessa blocked out Lizzie and all the sights and sounds around her. She was not going to be distracted—not now, when it was so important. She heard more—*roof, danger, help*—again and again, and realized it was Tiny. No, not only Tiny—it was all the animals at the shelter. They were in trouble.

Tessa grabbed Lizzie's arm. "There's some sort of emergency at the animal shelter. Don't ask me how I know. I just do."

"Let's go," said Lizzie without hesitation. "I'll let Penny know so she can get over there, too." She paused. "And I'm calling 911. Just in case."

Who is Nina Wonwon? Tessa wondered. *And what does she have to do with anything?* But it didn't matter. They just had to get to the shelter.

The girls raced down block after block. Tessa had no

idea where they were going, but Lizzie led her through back alleys and side streets to save time. "My mom hates when I take these shortcuts," Lizzie panted, "especially when it's getting dark. But it's the quickest way."

Tessa nodded, trying to save her breath.

They reached the shelter just as Penny's car squealed into the driveway. Tessa saw a large red vehicle with ladders on the sides pull up beside her, lights flashing and sirens squealing.

It's chaos here, Tessa thought, trying to take it all in. People jumped off the truck, wearing funny hats and heavy black raincoats and boots. Tessa was too concerned about the animals to pay those people much mind. She started to run to the door, but Penny leaped out of the car and pulled her back. "No! We can't go in yet."

"We have to," Tessa cried. "The poor animals!"

She turned to Lizzie, beside her, pale with concern. "Tiny! Snuggles!"

"I know," Lizzie said.

Just then a man came over. "I'm the fire captain," he said.

Fire captain? Tessa blinked. There wasn't a fire. That was clear.

"Everyone needs to stay outside until we make sure it's safe," the captain said. "I'm sending my crew in now."

More than anything, Tessa wanted to go, too. The thoughts in her head had quieted, and she didn't know what was going on. She stared at the animal shelter building. Part of the roof had caved in, right in the middle. It looked like someone had taken a giant shovel and scooped out the shingles. Again, she started forward. This time, the fire captain held her back.

"Stay here, young lady."

"It looks like most of the damage is over the lobby," Penny said. "That's good." She sighed. "That darn roof. I should have known there'd be trouble after the storm last night."

The captain's communication device squawked. He listened, then said, "The animals are okay. The place seems secure. But we can't be sure."

"We still need to get the animals out," Penny said determinedly. "There are other shelters nearby. We can divide them up until we decide what to do."

Yes, Tessa thought. *Yes, a plan.*

Penny turned to Tessa and Lizzie. "You two call volunteers and staff and organize a car- and vanpool." She handed her phone over with the contact list on the screen.

Tessa whipped out her Star-Zap, ready. While she and Lizzie made calls, the firefighters began to bring out the animals.

Then she heard Tiny's voice. He was thinking, *Watch out!* She couldn't take it anymore!

Tessa raced through the door, then stopped short. The lobby was flooded. Beams had fallen across the desk and the donation table. Bits of plaster sprinkled down. Looking up, she could see the sky.

A firefighter was just stepping into the room, carrying Tiny. The big dog squirmed out of his arms and raced to Tessa, almost knocking her over. Quickly, she took him outside. "You stay right here," she said, leading him down the path. Then she went again to the door, where another firefighter handed over a small puppy. She held him tightly, carrying him away.

"We should bring them to the dog run," she told the captain, "and get the leashes, too." Penny agreed. And as other volunteers and staff arrived, along with Lizzie's parents, they formed an animal-rescue brigade, passing dogs, cats, and cages from one pair of arms to another in a relay to safety.

Hours passed. Someone brought over pizza for dinner. By then, most of the animals had been delivered to other shelters. Only Tiny and Snuggles remained, refusing to budge from Tessa's side. "I want to take them home so badly," Lizzie whispered to her. "But we're leaving tomorrow. I just can't."

Tessa's heart sped. She had to complete her mission before time ran out. But she had to take care of Tiny and Snuggles, too. She turned to Penny and said, "You should take Tiny and Snuggles home with you."

"I should take Tiny and Snuggles home with me," Penny dutifully repeated. Then she added, "You and Lizzie, her parents, and anyone else who wants to should come to my place. We can discuss more plans. Yesterday I bought lots of raisin cinnamon buns. So we can have dessert, too."

CHAPTER
10

A small group was gathered at Penny's apartment. They were snacking on buns, making lists, and figuring things out. Penny was calculating the shelter's budget on her laptop, hoping to find money somewhere to fix the roof.

"Do you have an emergency fund?" Mrs. Bennett asked.

"We used that a few months ago to replace the wiring. Remember, Lizzie, when we had the power outage?"

Immediately, Tessa's thoughts flashed to the power outages at Starling Academy and the odd thing she thought she had heard Lady Cordial say. She had to make this wish come true so she could return home to find out what in the stars was going on.

Me, me. Tiny sent the thought straight to Tessa as he nosed her palm.

Tessa wished she had a treat for Tiny, a doggy snack or a bone. Maybe they could stop off at the general store again and pick up some things. The shop owner had been so nice, giving Lizzie a bone for Fiona. Tessa felt sure she'd be happy to help Tiny.

Suddenly, Tessa jumped to her feet. Maybe she would even donate to the shelter!

"We should let people know about the roof," she said. "Shopkeepers, neighbors. They'd probably want to help."

Penny snapped her fingers. "You're right! We can do a fund-raiser. Something quick and easy, online."

Lizzie leaned forward eagerly. "Yes! We can reach out to so many more people that way, not only in Hillsboro!"

"I'm going to set it up right now," said Penny. Tessa and Lizzie peeked over her shoulder as she pulled it all together, adding a link to the website and a donation tracker with a thermometer chart to measure incoming pledges. A green bar would rise with every donation until they reached their goal.

"We can post about it, too," Lizzie suggested, "and tell people to check the site."

"That's a good idea, honey," said her dad. "But we

really need to get going. I'm sorry we can't stay longer," he told Penny. "We have to be ready to leave by tomorrow afternoon."

It was late, so everyone went their separate ways, promising to meet back at Penny's apartment early the next morning.

"I'll stop by, too, first thing." Lizzie glanced at her parents to make sure it was okay. "So I can say good-bye—again!—before we go. And I'll write those donation posts when I get home."

That night, Tessa again set up her tent in the shelter's dog run. It made her feel better to be nearby, just in case something else happened to the shelter. She spent a restless night. And the next morning—after a quick breakfast of slightly stale astromuffins and mushy starberries— she hurried over to Penny's, hoping it wasn't too early.

Luckily, the shelter director was up and dressed and happy to see her. "You're the first one here," she told Tessa. "The last time I checked the donations thermometer, we hadn't raised much. But let's look right now."

She tapped a few keys on her laptop and gasped.

"What?" said Tessa, straining to see the screen.

Penny turned the laptop to face her, and then Tessa gasped, too. The donations had topped their goal!

"Let's see where all these came from," Penny said,

hitting some more keys. She looked over the page. "Hmmm. There are some local donations. But most of the pledges are from places I've never heard of, and lots from out of the country, too."

"Really?" Tessa peered at the laptop. London, England. Bridgetown, Barbados. Victoria Falls, Zimbabwe. Zurich, Switzerland. The names sounded vaguely familiar. Why would she even know them? Then she realized they were places Lizzie had lived.

Lizzie's friends had come through! Excited, Tessa read some of their posts: "Remembering our good times volunteering at the Zurich shelter, and your friendship. Love, Sonja." "This is for you, Lizzie. Come back to Barbados soon. Pamela." And one from Lizzie's dear friend Nola: "London isn't the same without you. Happy to help any way I can. xx Nola."

This was starmazing! The shelter would get a new roof. The animals could move back to a safe place. And even more starmendous? This could make Lizzie's wish come true. Once Lizzie realized she had loyal friends around the world, she'd see that moving so often was a blessing in disguise. That was the one good thing!

She wanted to tell Lizzie in person, so she texted: COME TO PENNY'S PLACE QUICK! GOOD NEWS!

In the meantime, other shelter workers arrived. The

room buzzed with excitement. *Where is Lizzie?* Tessa wondered, growing anxious. If she didn't come soon, she wouldn't be able to come at all. It was almost afternoon, and Lizzie had a flight to catch.

Just then the doorbell rang. "I'll get it!" Tessa cried, rushing for the door. She swung it open.

"Oh," she said, disappointed. "It's you."

"Gee," said Adora, standing on the other side, her hand on her hip. "Star greetings to you, too."

Tessa pulled Adora inside and gave her a quick hug. "I was just expecting my Wisher, that's all. And if you had waited a starhour or so, I would have finished my mission—successfully, I might add—and been on my merry way."

"Well," Adora noted, "we can't actually see what's happening here. We just know when a mission is in trouble. Lady Cordial wasn't kidding. Lady Stella admitted to us that there is a wish energy crisis. She said she didn't want to worry us, that's why she kept it a secret. But now everyone is going supernova, thinking Lady Stella is hiding something. And frankly, it seemed like you could use all the help you could get. Besides, maybe I can still make a difference."

"Maybe," Tessa said doubtfully. Adora looked like a muted version of herself, but her eyes were still an exquisite shade of sky blue, and really, Tessa was thrilled to see her.

How funny to see the Starling she basically shared a home with there when her Wisher was upset about leaving *her* home.

Quickly, she filled Adora in on Lizzie, the shelter, and the situation.

Adora shook her head. "Your Wisher sounds like a very emotional Wishling. I hope this isn't clouding your judgment, Tessa. Are you sure you have all the facts?"

"Yes, I have the facts!" Tessa said forcefully. "And once Lizzie gets here, you can analyze the situation yourself." *Hopefully*, she added to herself, *that will be soon.*

The Starlings were still standing just inside the door, not quite arguing, when the bell rang again. This time it was Lizzie.

"Lizzie!" Tessa cried. "Listen—" She stopped. Lizzie's eyes were swollen. Her skin was blotchy and her mouth quivered. Clearly, she'd been crying.

"Don't be upset! You don't have to worry anymore!" Tessa told her excitedly.

"Ahem," Adora said.

"Oh, this is my room—I mean, my friend Adora. She came to surprise me from . . . from my old hometown. After she heard about the shelter."

"Hi," said Lizzie, trying to smile. "It's nice that you came to help."

"See?" said Adora, turning to Tessa. "Everyone knows why I'm here!"

"But that's just it!" Tessa exclaimed. "I don't need— I mean, we don't need—any more help. We've gotten enough donations to build a new roof!"

"Really?" Lizzie's smile turned genuine. "That's incredible." Then she burst into tears.

"Are you okay?" Adora asked. She shot a look at Tessa.

"No!" Lizzie shook her head furiously. "Fiona is missing. We can't find her anywhere. And we're leaving soon! What are we going to do?" She flung her arms around Tessa, then reached into her pocket. "Look!" She pulled out Fiona's favorite chew toy, a squishy pink pig that oinked when you pressed it. "She doesn't even have Mr. Piggy!" she wailed.

Tessa reached out to hold hands with Lizzie. Then she asked Lizzie to recite a mantra with her. Lizzie looked at her through her tears, thoroughly confused.

"I think it will make us both feel better," Tessa told her.

A moment later, the two girls said, "Let your heart lead the way."

Almost immediately, Lizzie calmed down.

"We'll find Fiona," Tessa promised, feeling energized.

She quickly told Penny and the others, and soon everyone was working to find the lost dog. They made LOST DOG posters. They called friends. They set up search parties.

When they went back for a break, they saw Lizzie in the corner, talking on her phone. "Any news?" asked Tessa.

"No! And I have to go!" she told them. "My parents just told me the moving truck is here."

Tiny bounded over just then, wanting attention. Absentmindedly, Tessa scratched him behind one ear. She looked at him a moment and said, "Oh, the other ear is itchy." She paused. "And your tummy, too?" Tiny wagged his tail and rolled on the floor.

Meanwhile, Penny took Lizzie to the kitchen for a cup of soup before she left.

"How did you know the—what is it? a dog?—wanted to be petted that way?" Adora whispered to Tessa. "It seemed like you knew what he was thinking."

"I can get glimpses of his thoughts, and some other animals', too," Tessa explained. "It's my special talent."

"Can you do it with Fiona?" Adora asked.

Tessa grabbed her arm. "Adora! I am starmendously glad you're here. I don't know if it will work, but I can try. Maybe if I had something of hers . . ." Her voice trailed off; then she raced into the kitchen.

Lizzie sat at the table, oblivious to everything around her, spooning up her soup. Mr. Piggy was propped up next to the cup. Tessa picked up the toy and held it tightly, picturing Fiona as clearly as she could. *Where are you?* she thought, trying to send a message.

There was no answer.

Tessa moved Mr. Piggy closer to her heart. She poured her love of animals into the little pig. Suddenly, she felt a jolt of energy course through her body, out her tingling fingertips, and straight to Mr. Piggy. For a moment, his pink nose glowed.

Tessa closed her eyes and felt something. Fiona was safe, waiting patiently for Lizzie to find her. But where?

Tessa concentrated harder. A small slit of light was falling on Fiona's head. Soft, warm material surrounded her tiny body.

And that was all. Tessa groaned. It wasn't enough.

"We'll keep looking," Penny was telling Lizzie. "And I'll find a way to get her to your new home. But right now, you really need to go."

"Come on," said Tessa. "Adora and I will take you"— she almost said home but stopped herself—"back to your parents."

Outside Lizzie's house, a huge moving truck was parked at the curb. Workers carried boxes and hefted furniture, taking everything up a ramp to the rear of the truck. Lizzie peeked in. "It's full already!"

She rushed inside, shouting, "Mom! Dad! I'm not going without Fiona!"

"Oh, honey." Mr. Bennett wrapped his arms around her. "We can't stay much longer. Our flight leaves in a few hours."

"We're so sorry, Lizzie." Her mom wiped away her own tears. "We'd wait if we could."

Tessa felt terrible. Lizzie didn't want to go to begin with, but to move without her best friend must be unthinkable.

"I know I'm acting like a baby," Lizzie said, sniffling, "but I can't do this without Fiona."

The name Fiona echoed in Tessa's head, and suddenly, she could hear Fiona's thoughts: *I don't want to be left behind. I don't want to be left behind.* She saw more of Fiona's surroundings, too: something that looked like a book . . . a brush . . . a soft, fuzzy sweater . . .

"It's hard for all of us," Mrs. Bennett said. "But the truck is ready. Do you have everything?"

"Yes," Lizzie said in a trembling voice. "There's just my travel suitcase left. And I'm taking that on the plane."

"That's it!" Tessa cried. "Fiona is in your suitcase!"

Everyone raced up to Lizzie's room. The suitcase was on the floor, the top opened just a bit. Lizzie reached in, cried out in delight, and held up a wriggling, joyful Fiona.

"She was waiting in the suitcase," Tessa said, "to make sure you took her with you!"

"You silly dog," Lizzie gently scolded. "I would never leave you."

Lizzie's parents stroked Fiona, too, then left to talk to the movers. Grinning, Lizzie reached over to hug Tessa. "I am so happy! Thank you for being such a good friend."

Friend! With all the excitement about Fiona, Tessa had forgotten about Lizzie's friends' donations.

"I'm not your only good friend," she told Lizzie. "Do you know why the shelter raised so much money?"

Lizzie shook her head. "Because of you—and your friends from all over the world!" Tessa said, pulling up a screen on her Star-Zap showing all the messages from every corner of the planet. "Isn't it incredible? And you wouldn't have these friendships—not any of them!—if you hadn't moved around so much."

"It all adds up," Adora said in her cool, clear way.

"These friends are an important part of your life. A part you'd never want to miss out on."

Slowly, Lizzie nodded.

They were so close to granting the wish.

"And your friends in Hillsboro will never forget you, either," Tessa added. "You've done so much for the shelter! Penny is going to put a plaque in the new lobby, thanking you. And it's all because you moved here to Hillsboro!"

"Really?" Lizzie grinned.

A rainbow of colored lights flew from Lizzie, arcing through the air, then whooshing straight into Tessa's Wish Pendant. Lizzie's wish had come true! And Tessa had the wish energy to prove it.

She and Adora were grinning at each other like idiots when Lizzie's phone beeped. It was Penny, texting a special good-bye. Unbelievably, it seemed to Tessa, she wanted to let her know something else: she had decided to keep Tiny and Snuggles for her very own.

Now Tessa was feeling pretty emotional herself! Still, she wanted to do one more thing for Lizzie before she forgot. She grabbed a pen and wrote out some tips she'd come up with earlier for creating a homey space wherever you are: *Make sure you have the softest, most luxurious blanket. Your sheets should have the highest thread count. Put framed photos everywhere.*

"I envy you," she told Lizzie. "You get to make your room up all over again!" Then she winked at Adora and whispered softly, "But I wouldn't change mine for all the Zing on Starland." In fact, just thinking about their room—a jumble of cooking utensils and science equipment—made Tessa long for home.

Still, her mission had been starmazing. "Oh, Lizzie! I'll never forget you—or Fiona!"

Adora lifted her eyebrows and pointedly looked at at Tessa.

"Okay," said Tessa. "You have to go." She hugged Lizzie one last time. When they pulled apart, Lizzie looked at her a little strangely.

"Are you with the movers?" she asked. "I didn't know it was a family company."

Tessa thought of Gemma—and the other Star Darlings—and another wave of homesickness swept over her. "Yes," she said. "We are definitely a family that works together."

Then she added in a businesslike voice, "Just thought I'd come upstairs to make sure you have everything you need."

Lizzie hugged Fiona. "I sure do."

Tessa smiled and picked up one last thought as she and Adora left: *Bye, Tessa.*

It was sad that Lizzie would never remember her, but maybe Fiona would.

Epilogue

In no time at all, it seemed, she and Adora were back on Starland. At least, she assumed Adora was, too. Their stars had taken different courses. Just to be sure, she holo-texted: WHERE ARE YOU?

RIGHT OUTSIDE THE DORM! Adora responded in a starsec. ARE YOU COMING BACK TO THE ROOM?

I'M IN FRONT OF ILLUMINATION LIBRARY, Tessa holo-texted back. She was, in fact, in one of her favorite places: the sunlit library courtyard. It was a secluded, quiet place, filled with bluebeezle flowers and humming glitterbees. I'LL SEE YOU IN A LITTLE BIT, she added.

It felt nice to be alone, to run through everything that had happened in her mind and get her thoughts in order.

Unfortunately, someone else was rushing toward the courtyard. Then she grinned. It was Gemma!

"Tessa!" exclaimed Gemma. "I had a feeling I'd find you here!"

Tessa hugged her sister tightly. "For once, don't talk!" she warned. "I want to tell you about my mission. My Wisher made me think of you, and—"

Before she could say another word, their Star-Zaps buzzed.

"Wish Orb presentation time!" Gemma crowed. The girls linked arms and walked quickly to Lady Stella's office.

The ceremony was brief yet satisfying. The Star Darlings still looked uncomfortable around Lady Stella. But the headmistress was as warm as ever, even if she seemed a little distracted.

Tessa didn't want a lot of speeches or applause. At least, that's what she told herself. It was just nice to be acknowledged—and to see the orb transform into a Wish Blossom and then a Power Crystal. When the lovely vertessema spun its golden wheel, Tessa's Power Crystal fell right into her hand. It was a delicate gossamer crystal.

"How could someone so sweet be evil?" she whispered to Scarlet.

"To throw you off," Scarlet whispered back harshly.

Lady Stella cleared her throat, then glided out of the room. The girls rose, too, saying their last star congratulations to Tessa. Soon she was alone.

Well, that's that, thought Tessa, stepping out of the office and rounding a corner.

"Pssssst!" An arm shot out from a doorway and pulled her into a dark, empty room.

"What in the stars?" said Tessa.

"Hush, Tessa," someone said. Tessa recognized the voice. It was Cassie. Tessa's eyes adjusted to the gloom and she realized Scarlet was standing there, too.

"We're going down to the caves again," Scarlet said. "We tried to explore more while you were gone, but something always came up."

"One time Lady Stella called an extra SD class at the last starmin," explained Cassie. "It was like she knew what we were planning and wanted to stop us."

"And another time we were already in the supply closet, about to open the trapdoor, when Lady Cordial poked her head in to ask us to move furniture from the Lightning Lounge to the library," Scarlet added. "Why she couldn't just ask some Bot-Bots, I haven't the starriest."

"Still," Cassie said, "it was fun to practice wish

energy manipulation with heavy objects." She held back a giggle. "I just wish Lady Cordial hadn't told me to put that chair down right when it was hovering over her foot!"

Scarlet pulled up her hood and started for the door. "Enough chitchat. Let's go."

The three girls made their way to the supply closet, down the trapdoor steps, then into the cool, damp tunnels.

"I just know these caves hold some clues," Cassie whispered. "Stars crossed, this time we'll get lucky."

Tessa nodded, even though she really wanted to go to her room and take a sparkle shower. She had just come back from Wishworld, for star's sake, and here she was traipsing around these dim tunnels like she had all the startime in the worlds.

But still, she had to be there. Who else would be on the lookout for clues that proved Lady Stella innocent? Not that she didn't trust Cassie and Scarlet . . . well, at least Cassie.

Just a little way in, a bitbat swooped directly in front of them, and the Starlings stopped short.

"Why, hello there, little one," Scarlet said softly.

Tessa recognized the bitbat—or thought she did,

anyway—as the one who had met them the last time. Scarlet's special pet.

The bitbat fluttered her wings a star inch from Scarlet's nose, then seemed to beckon with one wing.

"Let's follow her," said Scarlet. "It's better than wandering around aimlessly."

Tessa and Cassie agreed. They walked single file through one tunnel after another, then another still, the bitbat leading the way. The tunnels grew narrower and more twisting as they sloped deeper underground. Tessa shivered. The air was colder, too.

She wasn't sure they could ever find their way out.

"I'm not enjoying this," she said. She thought of her cozy dorm room, where the temperature was always set at a perfect ten degrees Starrius. This definitely had none of the comforts of home.

Finally, the bitbat stopped, hovering in front of a sheer stone wall.

Tessa squinted. "This looks like any other part of the tunnels," she said as the bitbat dipped her head in farewell and disappeared into the darkness. "Why did she bring us here?" Her voice rose a bit in panic. "And how are we going to get out?"

"Let's take things one step at a time," Cassie said calmly.

"Yes, Tessa," said Scarlet testily. "Don't overreact here."

Tessa had to laugh. Scarlet was usually the one to act without thinking.

Just laughing made Tessa feel better. So she took her time, peering closely at the wall. "There's a crack here," she told the others. "It doesn't look like erosion or just some random break. It forms a perfect rectangle."

She traced her finger along the line, and the gray stone faded away to reveal a screen.

"A hidden holo-screen!" Cassie breathed.

The screen lit up suddenly, and Tessa blinked in the bright light. "Moons and stars!" she exclaimed.

"Password denied," said a Bot-Bot as the same words appeared on-screen.

Tessa gasped and pulled the others a little farther away. "Don't say anything too loudly," she warned. "It can hear us."

"There must be a secret room behind this wall. We have to come up with the password," Scarlet whispered excitedly. "I just know this could lead to answers!"

"We need to be careful, though," Cassie said in a low voice. "What if it's like one of those old stories, and we only get three tries? And if we're wrong, a stinkberry grows on our nose?"

"Oh, don't be such a scaredy-bitbat." Scarlet scoffed quietly. Then she faced the screen and, before Tessa or Cassie could stop her, shouted, "Lady Stella!"

"Password denied." The screen blinked.

"If it's three tries and we're out, we're already done here," Cassie said. "Should we chance it?"

"We have no choice." Tessa suddenly felt determined to see it through. "How about 'Star Darlings'?"

"I'll take this one." Scarlet edged to the holo-screen. "Star Darlings!"

Tessa tensed, expecting bells and alarms and stars knew what. Instead, the Bot-Bot just repeated, "Password denied."

"Well, at least we can keep trying," said Cassie.

The girls shouted out random words, willing to try anything.

"Wishlings. Bot-Bots!" "Wishworld!" Scarlet even tried "Secret password." But nothing worked.

Tessa's stomach rumbled. Not only had she gone straight from Wishworld to Lady Stella's office to the caves, but she hadn't even had time for a real meal.

"Moonberries!" she cried in annoyance.

The wall slid open. Tessa giggled. But then she grew sober as she recalled how much Lady Stella loved moonberries. Did that mean she had set up this secret room? And what would they find inside?

Holding hands, the girls edged inside the dark room. As soon as they crossed the threshold, the walls lit up brightly.

It was a small space, filled floor to ceiling with holo-books neatly placed on shelves. "Maybe it's just a storeroom for the library," Tessa said hopefully. Neither Scarlet nor Cassie bothered to reply.

Scarlet stepped up to a shelf and pulled out a holo-book. It looked extremely faded and worn. "This must be really, really old. Look—it's called *A History of Prism*. The town isn't even called Old Prism here."

"And look at this one," Cassie said, pulling another book from a shelf. "This one has all these old maps." She flipped the pages. "Here's the area around the Crystal Mountains. There's no Starling Academy!"

Tessa leaned closer. "The writing is so strange. All squiggly and hard to read." She reached for another book. "Most of these must be ancient!"

They browsed more shelves, and finally, Tessa pulled out a thick, heavy tome. Its deep purple cover had a glowing star, and Tessa sensed its power. If there had ever been a title, it had faded long before. She undid the heavy clasp.

Cassie and Scarlet watched as she thumbed through the pages. She stopped toward the end as a holo-picture came to life.

Twelve figures, clearly girls, posed in a circle. Glowing Wish Blossoms formed at their fingertips, swirling to meet in a burst of light. Dim words, difficult to read, were projected in the air.

"It says something about an oracle, a prophecy about the future," Cassie said, deciphering the text.

Haltingly, Tessa read phrases out loud: "'Twelve star-charmed Starlings' . . . 'Girls with a unique ability to grant wishes' . . . 'and so release wish energy so powerful' . . . 'save Starland' . . ." Her voice trailed off.

"The rest is a blur," Cassie said. Then she looked at Tessa and Scarlet. They gazed at one another in shock as understanding dawned on each of them.

"Oh my stars," said Tessa. "There are twelve girls in the prophecy. And there are twelve Star Darlings. The prophecy must be about us!"

Scarlet grinned. "I knew I was—I mean, we were—special!"

Just then the door closed with a whoosh.

The girls rushed to it. There was no screen on that side of the door. No hand scanner to slide it open. The stone was as smooth as polished glass.

With all her wish energy, Tessa willed the stone to crack, the door to open. Cassie and Scarlet did the same. It wouldn't budge.

They were trapped.

Glossary

Afterglow: The Starling afterlife. When Starlings die, it is said that they have "begun their afterglow."

Age of Fulfillment: The age at which a Starling is considered mature enough to begin to study wish granting.

Astromuffin: A delicious baked breakfast treat.

Bad Wish Orbs: Orbs that are the result of bad or selfish wishes made on Wishworld. These grow dark and warped and are quickly sent to the Negative Energy Facility.

Big Dipper Dormitory: Where third- and fourth-year students live.

Bitbat: A small winged nocturnal creature.

Bluebeezle: Delicate bright blue flowers that emit a scent only glitterbees can detect.

Blushbelle: A pink flower with a sweetly spicy scent.

Bot-Bot: A Starland robot. There are Bot-Bot guards, waiters, deliverers, and guides on Starland.

Bright Day: The date a Starling is born, celebrated each year like a Wishling birthday.

Celestial Café: Starling Academy's outstanding cafeteria.

Chickadoodle: A fluffy feathered farm creature that crows at sunrise and is similar to a Wishworld rooster.

Cocomoon: A sweet and creamy fruit with an iridescent glow.

Comet cake: A sweet Starland cake decorated to look like a comet, with a tail made of starberries.

Cosmic Transporter: The moving sidewalk system that transports students through dorms and across the Starling Academy campus.

Countdown Clock: A timing device on a Starling's Star-Zap. It lets them know how much time is left on a Wish Mission, which coincides with when the Wish Orb will fade.

Crystal Mountains: The most beautiful mountains on Starland. They are located across the lake from Starling Academy.

Cycle of Life: A Starling's life span. When Starlings die, they are said to have "completed their Cycle of Life."

Delicata: A sweet and fragrant liquid made by glitterbees and often used in baking.

Dododay: The third day of the starweek. The days in order are Sweetday, Shineday, Dododay, Yumday, Lunaday, Bopday, Reliquaday, and Babsday. (Starlandians have a three-day weekend every starweek.)

Druderwomp: An edible barrel-like bush capable of pulling up its own roots and rolling like a tumbleweed, then planting itself again.

Flutterfocus: A Starland creature similar to a Wishworld butterfly but with illuminated wings.

Galliope: A sparkly Starland creature similar to a Wishworld horse.

Garble greens: A Starland vegetable similar to spinach.

Glamera: A holographic image-recording device.

Glimmerworm: The larval stage of the glimmerbug. It spins a beautiful sparkly cocoon from its silk. "Pulling the glimmersilk over your eyes" is an expression meaning that someone is hiding something or is being deceptive.

Glitterbees: Blue-and-orange-striped bugs that pollinate Starland flowers and produce a sweet substance called delicata.

Glion: A gentle Starland creature similar in appearance to a Wishworld lion but with a multicolored glowing mane.

Glorange: A glowing orange fruit. Its juice is often enjoyed at breakfast time.

Glowfur: A small furry Starland creature with gossamer wings that eats flowers and glows.

Glowjay: A small flying animal with shimmering feathers.

Goldenella: A tall slender tree with golden blossoms that pop off the branches.

Good Wish Orbs: Orbs that are the result of positive wishes made on Wishworld. They are planted in Wish-Houses.

Halo Hall: The building where Starling Academy classes are held.

Holo-text: A message received on a Star-Zap and projected into the air. There are also holo-albums, holo-billboards, holo-books, holo-cards, holo-communications, holo-diaries, holo-flyers, holo-letters, holo-papers, holo-pictures, and holo–place cards. Anything that would be made of paper or contain writing or images on Wishworld is a hologram on Starland.

Hydrong: The equivalent of a Wishworld hundred.

Illumination Library: The impressive library at Starling Academy.

Impossible Wish Orbs: Orbs that are the result of wishes made on Wishworld that are beyond the power of Starlings to grant.

Lightning Lounge: A place on the Starling Academy campus where students relax and socialize.

Little Dipper Dormitory: Where first- and second-year students live.

Luminous Lake: A serene and lovely lake next to the Starling Academy campus.

Mirror Mantra: A saying specific to each Star Darling that when recited gives her (and her Wisher) reassurance and strength. When a Starling recites her Mirror Mantra while looking in a mirror, she will see her true appearance reflected.

Moogle: A very short but unspecific amount of time. The word is used in expressions like "Wait just a moogle!"

Moonberries: Sweet berries that grow on Starland. They are both Tessa's and Lady Stella's favorite snack.

Moonium: An amount similar to a Wishworld million.

Old Prism: A medium-sized historical city about an hour from Starling Academy.

Ozziefruit: Sweet plum-sized indigo fruit that grows on pink-leaved trees and is usually eaten raw or cooked in pies.

Power Crystal: The powerful stone each Star Darling receives once she has granted her first wish.

Quax: A unit of measurement used in cooking, similar to a cup.

Radiant Recreation Center: The building at Starling Academy where students take Physical Energy, health, and fitness classes. The rec center has a large gymnasium for exercising, a running track, areas for games, and a sparkling star-pool.

Serenity Islands: A Starland recreation area. Starlings sometimes take paddleboat rides around it.

Shimmer-butter: A delectable creamy spread that is often used on baked goods.

Solar Springs: Tessa and Gemma's hometown. A hilly and rural small town with few businesses and far-flung farms and ranches.

Shooting stars: Speeding stars that Starlings can latch on to and ride to Wishworld.

Sparkleberries: A Starland fruit that is used in baking and often included as an ingredient in comet cakes.

Sparkle shower: An energy shower Starlings take every day to get clean and refresh their sparkling glow.

Sparklesugar: An ingredient used to sweeten baked goods.

Starapple: A large crunchy and sweet Starland fruit that grows on Tessa and Gemma's farm.

Star ball: An intramural sport that shares similarities with soccer on Wishworld, but star ball players use energy manipulation to control the ball.

Starberries: Bright red berries that grow on Starland and are used to create the tails on comet cakes.

Starcar: The primary mode of transportation for most Starlings. These ultrasafe vehicles drive themselves on cushions of wish energy.

Star Caves: The caverns underneath Starling Academy where the Star Darlings' secret Wish-Cavern is located.

Starf!: A Starling expression of dismay.

Star flash: News bulletin, often used sarcastically.

Star Kindness Day: A special Starland holiday that celebrates spreading kindness, compliments, and good cheer.

Starland City: The largest city on Starland, also its capital.

Starlicious: Tasty, delicious.

Starlings: The glowing beings with sparkly skin who live on Starland.

Star Quad: The center of the Starling Academy campus. The dancing fountain, band shell, and hedge maze are located here.

Star sack: A Starland tote bag. This container starts about the size of a lunch bag, but it expands to hold whatever is stored inside.

Star salutations: The Starling way to say "thank you."

Staryear: A time period on Starland, the equivalent of a Wishworld year.

Star-Zap: The ultimate smartphone that Starlings use for all communications. It has myriad features.

Stellation: The point of a star. Halo Hall has five stellations, each housing a different department.

Sunflour: A baking ingredient made from ground-up plants. It is a basic ingredient of cakes and breads.

Supernova: A stellar explosion. Also used colloquially, meaning "really angry," as in "She went supernova when she found out the bad news."

Time of Letting Go: One of the four seasons on Starland. It falls between the warmest season and the coldest, similar to fall on Wishworld.

Time of Lumiere: The warmest season on Starland, similar to summer on Wishworld.

Time of New Beginnings: Similar to spring on Wishworld, this is the season that follows the coldest time of year; it's when plants and trees come into bloom.

Time of Shadows: The coldest season of the year on Starland, similar to winter on Wishworld.

Toothlight: A high-tech gadget Starlings use to clean their teeth.

Twinkelopes: Majestic herd animals. Males have imposing antlers with star-shaped horns, and females have iridescent manes and flowing tails.

Vertessema: Tessa's Wish Blossom. A wheel-shaped flower made of golden stars.

Wish Blossom: The bloom that appears from a Wish Orb after its wish is granted.

Wish energy: The positive energy that is released when a wish is granted. Wish energy powers everything on Starland.

Wisher: The Wishling who has made the wish that is being granted.

Wish-Granters: Starlings whose job is to travel down to Wishworld to help make wishes come true and collect wish energy.

Wish-House: The place where Wish Orbs are planted and cared for until they sparkle. Once the orb's wish is granted, it becomes a Wish Blossom.

Wishlings: The inhabitants of Wishworld.

Wish Mission: The task a Starling undertakes when she travels to Wishworld to help grant a wish.

Wish Orb: The form a wish takes on Wishworld before traveling to Starland. There it will grow and sparkle when it's time to grant the wish.

Wish Pendant: A gadget that absorbs and transports wish energy, helps Starlings locate their Wishers, and changes a Starling's appearance. Each Wish Pendant holds a different special power for its Star Darling.

Wishworld: The planet Starland relies on for wish energy. The beings on Wishworld know it by another name—Earth.

Wishworld Outfit Selector: A program on each Star-Zap that accesses

Wishworld fashions for Starlings to wear to blend in on their Wish Missions.

Wishworld Surveillance Deck: A platform located high above the campus, where Starling Academy students go to observe Wishlings through high-powered telescopes.

Zing: A traditional Starling breakfast drink. It can be enjoyed hot or iced.

Zingspoon: A small unit of measurement often used when baking, roughly equivalent to a Wishworld teaspoon.

Acknowledgments

It is impossible to list all of our gratitude, but we will try.

Our most precious gift and greatest teacher, Halo; we love you more than there are stars in the sky . . . punashaku. To the rest of our crazy, awesome, unique tribe—thank you for teaching us to go for our dreams. Integrity. Strength. Love. Foundation. Family. Grateful. Mimi Muldoon—from your star doodling to naming our Star Darlings, your artistry, unconditional love, and inspiration is infinite. Didi Muldoon—your belief and support in us is only matched by your fierce protection and massive-hearted guidance. Gail. Queen G. Your business sense and witchy wisdom are legendary. Frank—you are missed and we know you are watching over us all. Along with Tutu, Nana, and Deda, who are always present, gently guiding us in spirit. To our colorful, totally genius, and bananas siblings—Patrick, Moon, Diva, and Dweezil—there is more creativity and humor in those four names than most people experience in a lifetime. Blessed. To our magical nieces—Mathilda, Zola, Ceylon, and Mia—the Star Darlings adore you and so do we. Our witchy cuzzie fairy godmothers—Ane and Gina. Our fairy fashion godfather, Paris. Our sweet Panay. Teeta and Freddy—we love you all so much. And our four-legged fur babies—Sandwich, Luna, Figgy, and Pinky Star.

The incredible Barry Waldo, our SD partner. Sent to us from above in perfect timing. Your expertise and friendship are beyond words. We love you and Gary to the moon and back. Long live the manifestation room!

Catherine Daly—the stars shined brightly upon us the day we aligned with you. Your talent and inspiration are otherworldly; our appreciation cannot be expressed in words. Many heartfelt hugs for you and the adorable Oonagh.

To our beloved Disney family. Thank you for believing in us. Wendy Lefkon, our master guide and friend through this entire journey. Stephanie Lurie, for being the first to believe in Star Darlings. Suzanne Murphy, who helped every step of the way. Jeanne Mosure, we fell in love with you the first time we met, and Star Darlings wouldn't be what it is without you. Andrew Sugerman, thank you so much for all your support.

Our team . . . Devon (pony pants) and our Monsterfoot crew—so grateful. Richard Scheltinga—our angel and protector. Chris Abramson—thank you! Special appreciation to Richard Thompson, John LaViolette, Swanna, Mario, and Sam.

To our friends old and new—we are so grateful to be on this rad journey that is life with you all. Fay. Jorja. Chandra. Sananda. Sandy. Kathryn. Louise. What wisdom and strength you share. Ruth, Mike, and the rest of our magical Wagon Wheel bunch—how lucky we are. How inspiring you are. We love you.

Last—we have immeasurable gratitude for every person we've met along our journey, for all the good and the bad; it is all a gift. From the bottom of our hearts we thank you for touching our lives.

Shana Muldoon Zappa is a jewelry designer and writer who was born and raised in Los Angeles. She has an endless imagination and a passion to inspire positivity through her many artistic endeavors. She and her husband, Ahmet Zappa, collaborated on Star Darlings especially for their magical little girl and biggest inspiration, Halo Violetta Zappa.

Ahmet Zappa is the *New York Times* best-selling author of *Because I'm Your Dad* and *The Monstrous Memoirs of a Mighty McFearless*. He writes and produces films and television shows and loves pancakes, unicorns, and making funny faces for Halo and Shana.

Adora
finds a friend

"*Mmmmmm, hmmmm, mmmmm, hmmmm.*" Adora hummed tunelessly, alone in her dorm room.

It felt nice to have the room all to herself. Still, it was a little strange that Tessa, her roommate, wasn't there.

The two had just come back from a Wish Mission. It was Tessa's mission; Adora had yet to be chosen for her own mission to Wishworld. But Adora had been sent to help when the situation looked dim. Of course, she'd quickly put in her two starcents. Really, Tessa had been so caught up in her Wisher's emotions that she couldn't see the orchard for the ozziefruit trees. Luckily, Adora had set her straight. So, thank the stars, the trip had been successful and really quite exciting.

After the SD ceremony, where Tessa had gotten her Power Crystal, Adora had expected her to come straight back to their room. Tessa was quite the homebody after all. And there were her virtual galliope, Jewel, to feed and her micro-zap waiting to bake yummy astromuffins.

But Tessa hadn't so much as stopped off at the room as far as Adora could tell. Probably, Adora reasoned, she was catching up with her younger sister, Gemma. And Adora planned to take full advantage of her alone time.

Adora had been right in the middle of an experiment when she'd been called on to help Tessa. She'd been itching to get back to it for over a starday now. It combined her two biggest passions: science and fashion. Specifically, sequins.

Adora wanted to make sequins—disc-shaped shiny beads—extra twinkly. That alone wouldn't be so difficult. But she wanted that newfound sparkle to bring out each sequin's color, too, to make the shades themselves brighter, warmer, more radiant.

The gold sequins that Leona favored had to become even more brightly golden; Cassie's silver ones even more silvery; Clover's an even deeper, more brilliant purple. And Adora's goal was to do it with just one formula.

She wanted the formula to work with every shade

under the suns, and that was twelve in the Star Darlings group alone. Add in all the different tones at Starling Academy, or furthermore all of Starland itself, and the numbers were star-boggling!

Adora had already removed natural elements from glittery yellow calliope flowers, fiery red florafierces, and other plants and trees. Now she needed to add twinkle-oxide—with a spark of glowzene for good measure—into each mixture. The combination had to be just right, so the formula would react with any Starling shade.

Luckily, it was Bopday, the first starday of the weekend, which left her plenty of time to test her ideas. Adora would be logical and methodical as always. But she wanted to get it done sooner rather than later, so the sequins could be sewn onto outfits the Star Darlings band members planned to wear for a big competition.

"*Mmmmm, hmmm, mmmmm.*" Adora hummed, pouring 5.6 lumins of twinkle-oxide into a beaker. "*Mmmm, hmmmmm.*" She turned on her personal bright-burner to 179 degrees Starrius and waited for the mixture to heat. "*Mmmm.*"

Alone in the room, Adora felt free to sing to her heart's content. Her own music skills were nothing to brag about, but Adora wasn't much into the arts anyway. For her, it was science, science, science—and fashion, fashion, fashion.

Adora planned to be a style scientist, maybe the first in all of Starland. And she'd show the worlds she was the brightest in both.

Adora's parents owned a trendy clothing store in Radiant Hills, the ultraexclusive community in Starland City, where Libby had grown up alongside glimmerous celebrighties and famous Starlandians.

Adora herself lived in a perfectly nice neighborhood of modest, comfortable homes. She couldn't complain. She and her parents shared a simple one-level house where they each had their own workspace, creating designs to sell in the store. Even as a wee Starling, she'd had a microscope and a star-sewing machine, creating lustrous new fabrics for her parents to work into clothing designs.

Concentrating now, Adora pushed back sky blue strands of hair that had fallen out of her loose bun and adjusted her knee-length glittery lab coat and gloves. She checked her pockets, making sure the extra test tubes she always carried around were closed up tight.

Finally, with great care, she straightened her safety

starglasses. She'd realized when she and Tessa were first years that safety came first.

Back then, Tessa had just mixed a batch of glowrange smoothies. Adora, meanwhile, had been working on fabric that would sparkle extra bright on the dreariest, rainiest days. She'd combined orangey lightning in a bottle with starfuric acid, and was ready to steep the fabric. The mixture did look a bit like the smoothies, Adora had to admit. So it was no wonder Tessa reached for it when a moonberry got caught in her throat. Adora had to make a running dive to knock the liquid out of her hands.

Right after that, Adora had established rules, including clearly separating food from experiments and wearing safety starglasses. That last part was particularly important, Adora realized a starsec later, when—

Bang! Her sequins mixture fizzled and sparked, overflowing from the beaker and spilling onto her workspace. Immediately, the smoking liquid disappeared, thanks to the self-cleaning technology featured in all Starland furnishings.

Adora's room in particular was squeaky clean and spare—some might say sterile and uninteresting—with a neat desktop and lab space, with carefully arranged beakers and test tubes. Even the "fashion section" had neat cubbies for bolts of fabrics and a carefully polished star-sewing machine.

She did like an orderly room, with minimal possessions. Tessa, on the other hand, had brought a moonium knickknacks—along with plants and herbs and old holo-cookbooks—from home when they first moved in together.

Adora didn't quite understand. She didn't get attached to things. Out with the old, in with the new, she thought frequently, deleting old experiment notes and equations. She was thinking that now, in fact, as she struck the sequins formula from her holo–lab notes.

"*Starf*," Adora said, eying the now blank screen. She'd have to start over, maybe lowering the bright-burner to 147 degrees. But that was okay. That was what science was all about—trial and error and patience.

And that was all part of the lightentific method, Adora's personal approach to experimenting:

Ask a question based on observation. Come up with a reasonable hypothesis (a guess, really) to answer the question. Create an experiment to see if the guess was correct, and analyze the results. Finally, draw a conclusion: either the experiment worked or it failed.

But Adora wasn't one to accept failure.

"*Mmmmmm!*" Adora's voice grew more powerful as

she started on a new hypothesis. It was a relief, really, to be loud. She'd talked in a whisper for so long—the effects of that poisonous nail polish— and had been so frustrated when people couldn't hear her! At least it had been better than giggling nonstop like Sage, though. Or pulling practical jokes like Astra had done. No one likes when drinks are switched at the Celestial Café!

Adora was carefully carrying fresh batches of mixture to the bright-burner when her Star-Zap buzzed.

Should she ignore it? Just keep concentrating on her experiment?

Part of her wanted to do just that. But with all the strange goings-on lately, it could be an important message. Or maybe it was an announcement for the next mission!

"Oh, moonberries," she said, using Tessa's favorite expression as she set down the beakers. She'd just have to check. She reached for her Star-Zap and glanced at the screen.

A group holo-letter from Cassie? she thought. That was a little bizarre. Why would Cassie write an entire letter when she could just talk to the Star Darlings or send a brief holo-text?

Adora tapped the screen and the letter appeared in the air, floating at eye-level. Quickly, she read the note, then read it again just to be sure: Cassie was with Tessa—and Scarlet—and they were trapped in the Star Caves. There Adora was, happily going about her experiment, pleased as sparkle-punch to have the room to herself, while Tessa had been in trouble the whole time.

Every problem had a solution—scientific, mathematical, or otherwise. It just took a cool, clear mind to figure it out. But Adora had to leave the room, step away from Tessa's knickknacks and holo-photos from the farm, to think things through. Calmly, she went outside.

"Adora! Thank the stars you're here!" Leona shouted, rushing down the hall, her golden curls flying behind her. "Did you see Cassie's holo-letter?"

"Shh!" hissed Adora. She glanced pointedly in the other direction, where two other third-years were getting off the Cosmic Transporter and eyeing them curiously.

"Just the SDs being SDish," one said with a laugh.

Ask just about any Starling Academy student and they would say SD stood for Slow Developers, a nickname given to the twelve girls because they all attended a special class for extra help. Little did the students know, however, that SD was also short for Star Darlings. And the "extra help" taught the girls how to travel to